Antoine Laurain was born in Paris and is a journalist, antiques collector and award-winning author. His novels include *The President's Hat* and *The Red Notebook*.

Jane Aitken is a publisher and translator from the French.

Emily Boyce is in-house translator and editor at Gallic Books.

Praise for *The President's Hat*:

'A hymn to *la vie Parisienne* ... enjoy it for its fabulistic narrative, and the way it teeters pleasantly on the edge of Gallic whimsy' *The Guardian*, Paperback of the Week

'A fable of romance and redemption' *The Telegraph*

'Its gentle satirical humor reminded me of Jacques Tati's classic films' *Library Journal*

'As entertaining as it is original, this is a story to enjoy like a chocolate with a surprise centre' *Marie France*

Praise for *The Red Notebook*:

'Resist this novel if you can; it's the very quintessence of French romance' *The Times*

'In equal parts an offbeat romance, detective story and a clarion call for metropolitans to look after their neighbours ... reading *The Red Notebook* is a little like finding a gem among the bric-a-brac in a local brocante' *The Telegraph*

'Soaked in Parisian atmosphere, this lovely, clever, funny novel will have you rushing to the Eurostar post-haste' *Daily Mail*

'An endearing love story written in beautifully poetic prose. It is an enthralling mystery about chasing the unknown, the nostalgia for what could have been, and most importantly, the persistence of curiosity' *San Francisco Book Review*

French Rhapsody

French Rhapsody

By Antoine Laurain

Translated from the French by Jane Aitken
and Emily Boyce

Gallic Books

London

This book is published with support from the 'Programmes d'aide
à la publication' of the Institut français

A Gallic Book

First published in France as *Rhapsodie française*
by Éditions Flammarion, 2016
Copyright © Éditions Flammarion, 2016
English translation copyright © Gallic Books 2016

First published in Great Britain in 2016 by Gallic Books,
59 Ebury Street, London, SW1W 0NZ

A CIP record for this book is available from the British Library
ISBN 978-1-910477-30-4

Typeset in Fournier MT and Calibri by Gallic Books
Printed and bound by CPI Group (UK) Ltd, Croydon, CR0 4YY

2 4 6 8 10 9 7 5 3 1

Within all of us there are secret things, obscure, profound impressions, which, like the rest of our previous existence or the glimmerings of a future life, are a sort of psychic dust, ash or seed, to be remembered or foreseen.

Henri de Régnier
Les Cahiers (1927)

Rhapsody:

In classical music, a rhapsody is a free composition for a solo instrument, several instruments or a symphony orchestra. Quite similar to a fantasia, a rhapsody almost always draws on national or regional themes.

A Letter

The assistant manager, a tired-looking little man with a narrow, greying moustache, had invited him to sit down in a tiny windowless office brightened only by its canary-yellow door. When Alain saw the carefully framed notice, he felt nervous laughter return – but more hysterical this time, and accompanied by the disagreeable feeling that if God existed, he had a very dubious sense of humour. The notice showed a joyful team of postmen and -women all giving the thumbs up. Running across the top in yellow letters were the words 'The future: brought to you by the Post Office.' Alain chuckled mirthlessly. 'Great slogan.'

'No need to be sarcastic, Monsieur,' replied the civil servant calmly.

'Don't you think I'm entitled to a little sarcasm?' demanded Alain, pointing to his letter. 'Thirty-three years late. How do you explain that?'

'Your tone is not helpful, Monsieur,' replied the man drily.

Alain glared at him. The assistant manager held his gaze for a moment, then slowly extended his arm towards a blue folder which he opened with some ceremony. Then he licked his finger and started turning the pages, rather slowly. 'And your name is?' he murmured, not looking at Alain.

'Massoulier,' replied Alain.

'Ah, yes, Dr Alain Massoulier, 38 Rue de Moscou, Paris

8ᵉ,' the civil servant read aloud. 'You're aware that we're modernising?'

'The results are impressive.'

The man with the moustache looked at Alain again in silence and seemed about to say something sharp, but apparently thought better of it.

'As I was saying, the building is being modernised, so all the wooden shelves, dating back to its construction in 1954, were taken down last week. The workmen found four letters which had fallen down the back and were trapped between the floor and the shelves. The oldest dated back to ... 1963,' he confirmed, reading from the file. 'Then there was a postcard from 1978, a letter from 1983 – that's yours – and lastly, a letter from 2002. We took the decision that, where possible, we would deliver them to their recipients if they were still alive and easily identifiable from their addresses. That's the explanation,' he said, closing the blue file.

'But no apology?' said Alain.

Eventually the assistant manager said, 'If you wish, we can send you our apology form letter. Would that be of use?'

Alain looked down at the desk where his eye fell on a heavy cast-iron paperweight, embellished with the insignia of the postal service. He briefly saw himself picking it up and hitting the little moustachioed man with it repeatedly.

'For whatever purpose it may serve,' droned the man, 'does this letter have a legal significance (with regard to an inheritance or transfer of shares or similar) such that the delay in delivery would activate legal proceedings against the postal service—'

'No, it does not,' Alain cut him off brusquely.

The man asked him for his signature at the bottom of a form that Alain did not even bother to read. Alain left and stopped outside in front of a skip. Workmen were throwing solid oak planks and metal structures into it, shouting at each other in what Alain believed was Serbian.

Passing a mirror in a chemist's window, Alain caught sight of his reflection. He saw grey hair and the rimless glasses that his optician claimed were as good as a facelift. An ageing doctor, that's what the mirror reflected back at him, an ageing doctor like so many thousands of others across the country. A doctor, just like his father before him.

Written on a typewriter and signed in turquoise ink, the letter had arrived in the morning post. In the top left-hand corner was the logo of the famous record label: a semicircle above the name, featuring a vinyl record in the form of a setting sun – or maybe a rising sun. The paper had yellowed at the edges. Alain had reread the letter three times before putting it back in the envelope. His name was correct, his address was correct. Everything was in order except for the date, 12 September 1983. That date was also printed over the stamp – a Marianne that had been out of circulation for a long time. The postmark was only half printed but you could clearly read: Paris – 12/9/83. Alain had suppressed a fleeting guffaw like an unwelcome tic. Then he had shaken his head, smiling incredulously. Thirty-three years. That letter had taken thirty-three years to travel across three *arrondissements* of the capital.

The day's post – an electricity bill, *Le Figaro*, *L'Obs*, three publicity flyers (one for a mobile phone, one for a travel agent and the third for an insurance company) – had just been brought up by Madame Da Silva, the concierge. Alain had considered getting up, opening the door and catching Madame Da Silva on the stairs to ask her where the letter had come from. But she would already be back downstairs in her apartment, and anyway, she wouldn't be able to help him. She had merely brought up what the postman had delivered to the building.

Paris, 12 September 1983

Dear Holograms
We listened with great interest to the five-track demo tape you sent us at the beginning of the summer. Your work is precise and very professional, and although it needs quite a bit of work, you already have a sound that is distinctive. The track we were most impressed by was 'Such Stuff as Dreams Are Made On'. You have managed to blend new wave and cold wave whilst adding your own rock sound.

Please get in touch with us so that we can organise a meeting.

Best wishes

Claude Kalan
ARTISTIC DIRECTOR

The tone was polite but friendly. Alain focused on the words 'precise' and 'very professional' whilst noting the slightly derogatory repetition of the word 'work'. And the letter ended on an encouraging note, an affirmation in fact. Yes, thought Alain, 'Such Stuff as Dreams Are Made On' was the best, a jewel, a hit, whispered in Bérengère's voice. Alain closed his eyes and recalled her face with almost surreal precision: her big eyes, always vaguely worried, her short haircut with the fringe sweeping over her forehead, the way she had of going up to the mic and holding it with both hands and not letting go for the whole song. She would close her eyes and the soft voice with its touch of huskiness was always a surprise coming from a girl of nineteen. Alain opened his eyes again: 'a meeting' – how many times had the five of them uttered that word. How many times had they hoped for a meeting with a record label: a meeting at eleven on Monday at our offices. We have a meeting at Polydor. That 'meeting' had never been forthcoming. The Holograms had split up. Although that was not exactly the right term. It would be more accurate to say that life had simply moved on, causing the group to disperse. In the absence of a response from any record label, they had each gone their own way, disappointed and tired of waiting.

Still half asleep in her blue silk dressing gown, Véronique had just pushed open the kitchen door. Alain looked up at her and handed her the letter. She read it through, yawning.

'It's a mistake,' she said.

'It certainly is not,' retorted Alain, holding out the envelope. 'Alain Massoulier, that's me.'

'I don't understand.' Véronique shook her head, indicating that untangling an enigma so soon after waking up was beyond her.

'The date, look at the date.'

She read out, '1983.'

'The Holograms, that was my group, my rock group. Well, it wasn't rock, it was new wave; cold wave to be exact, as it says here.' Alain pointed to the relevant line in the letter.

Véronique looked at her husband in astonishment.

'The letter took thirty-three years to travel across three *arrondissements.*'

'Are you sure?' she murmured, turning the letter over.

'Have you got another explanation?'

'You'll have to ask at the post office,' concluded Véronique, sitting down.

'I'm going to! I wouldn't miss that for the world,' replied Alain.

Then he got up and started the Nespresso machine.

'Make me one,' said Véronique, yawning again.

Alain thought it was time his wife cut down on the sleeping tablets. It was distressing to see her every morning appearing like a rumpled shrew. It would take her at least two hours in the bathroom before she emerged dressed and made up. So all in all it took nearly three hours for Véronique to get herself properly together. Since the children had left home, Alain and Véronique found themselves living on their own as at the beginning of their marriage. But twenty-five years had passed and what had seemed charming at the beginning was becoming a little wearing, and now long silences stretched out over dinner. In order to fill them Véronique talked about her clients and her latest decorative finds, while Alain would mention patients or colleagues, and then they would fall to discussing their holiday plans although they could never agree where to go.

Backache

Alain stayed in bed for a week. The day the letter had arrived, he'd been laid low with backache which he first diagnosed as lumbago, then sciatica, or maybe neuralgia. Or perhaps the cause was not medical at all. He hadn't carried anything heavy, or made a sudden movement and heard a suspicious crack. He couldn't exclude the possibility that the pain was psychosomatic. But whatever the cause, it didn't change the fact that he was lying in bed, in his pyjamas, with a hot-water bottle under his back. He was on painkillers and moved around the flat like an old man, taking little steps, with a look of suffering on his face. He had instructed his secretary, Maryam, to cancel all his appointments until further notice and then go home herself.

The day the letter arrived had seemed endless. Like some strange mirror effect the letter's thirty-three-year delay seemed to have infected the passage of time, causing it to slow down. At four o'clock, Alain felt as if he'd been in his consulting room listening to the ills of his patients for about fifteen hours. Every time he opened the door to the waiting room, it seemed to have filled up again. An outbreak of gastroenteritis was the reason for all the people. He had listened to dozens of accounts of diarrhoea and stomach cramps. 'I feel as if I'm going to shit my brains out, Doctor!' had been the colourful expression the local butcher had used. As Alain listened to him, he decided to stop buying meat from him.

The day should have passed in calm contemplation. You think you have buried your youthful dreams, that they've dissolved in the fog of passing years and then you realise it's not true! The corpse is still there, terrifying and unburied. He should have found a grave for it and something funereal should have followed his reading of the letter, funereal and silent, accompanied by incense. Instead, it seemed as if the entire city had made its way to his apartment to regale him with sordid tales of their intestines, their diarrhoea, and their flushing toilets.

Little Amélie Berthier, eight years old, had come with her mother. She didn't have a stomach bug, she had a sore throat and repeatedly refused to open her mouth. Sitting on the edge of the examination table, the little minx shied away, shaking her head, every time Alain approached with the disposable tongue depressor and torch.

'You must sit still,' he said sternly.

The child had calmed down immediately and let her throat be examined without any more fuss. Alain then wrote the prescription in heavy silence.

'She needs discipline,' her mother volunteered reluctantly.

'Possibly,' replied Alain coldly.

'But what can you expect with a father who's never there …' said the mother, leaving the sentence unfinished in the hope that the doctor would ask her about it.

Alain did not. After ushering them out, he allowed himself a few minutes' break, massaging his temples.

The surgery had ended at twenty past seven with a patient whose eczema had flared up again and who had come to add his contribution to the day. Before that there had been an earache, a urinary tract infection, several cases of bronchitis and more gastroenteritis. Alain had uttered the somewhat pompous phrase 'intestinal flora' several times. He had often noticed that patients with stomach bugs liked to be told they 'must boost their intestinal flora'. They always nodded gravely. Becoming the careful gardener of their insides was a project that gave them purpose. After accompanying his eczema patient to the door, Alain washed his hands thoroughly and then poured himself a strong whisky in the kitchen. He practically downed it in one. Then he went out to one of the cupboards in the corridor and started to empty it. Soon the iron, diving masks, files, beach towels, and folders of the children's schoolwork were spread all over the floor. He wanted to find an answer to the question that had been nagging at him all day – had he kept the shoebox containing his photos of the group and the cassette? He wasn't sure any more. He could clearly picture it on the upper shelf where it had been for years. Had he *planned* to throw it out or had he *actually* thrown it out? The assorted pile of little-used objects expanding on the carpet seemed to indicate the latter. It was maddening. The only thing Alain wanted to do at that precise moment was to put the tape into the old Yamaha cassette player and listen to the band again. And he especially wanted to hear 'Such Stuff as Dreams Are Made On'. The music and Bérengère's voice had been playing in his head all day.

'Idiot, idiot, idiot ...' muttered Alain. He must indeed have thrown it away. Now he remembered. He'd wanted to sort out the cupboard two or three years ago, over the long Easter weekend. He'd used a large bin bag and he must have chucked the box in without even opening it, in amongst the out-of-date bills and the old shoes no one wore any more. He had even thrown away things from his parents' time which hadn't been moved for years.

At the back of the cupboard, behind three overcoats, he spied the black case with Gibson on it and at his feet he saw the Marshall amplifier. He pulled the case out carefully and unzipped it. The black lacquer of the electric guitar was as shiny as ever; time had not taken its toll. Ten years ago his children had asked to see it and Alain had shown it to them although he had refused to play anything. They thought it was funny that not only did their father possess an electric guitar, but that he actually knew how to play it. Alain ran his fingers over the strings then quickly zipped up the cover and put the guitar back in the cupboard behind the winter coats. That was when he noticed his back was hurting. An hour later he was in bed.

Sweet Eighties

It had all started with an advert in *Rock & Folk*. 'New-wave band the Holograms and their singer Bérengère seek electric guitarist. Good standard required for young but motivated group. Come and audition before we get famous!' Alain had turned up at the appointed place: the garage of a house in Juvisy belonging to the parents of the bass guitarist who'd been recruited a few weeks earlier by the same method. That afternoon three boys tried out and Alain had been chosen after giving a rendition of part of Van Halen's 'Eruption', a bit of Queen, and Pink Floyd's 'Another Brick in the Wall'.

It's always the same with bands. A group of individuals with different aims get together united by a love of music. They play on their own at home and want to meet other guys and girls who also play on their own at home. They want to create the kind of sound that's not on the radio. They feel they've captured the essence of their era and they want to share it with their generation and more widely with that vast, mysterious entity called 'the general public'. The Beatles, the Rolling Stones, Indochine and Téléphone all started like that – with an advert, a meeting and a stroke of luck. At that time when you still have your whole life ahead of you, when the field of possibilities seems wide open, at that age when you can't for a moment imagine being fifty-two – even the thought of it seems a fantasy. You're going to be twenty for eternity and beyond, and what's more, you are exactly what the world is waiting for. As a general rule, you are still untouched by tragedy: you still have your parents; your life, and that of those around you, is stable. Everything is possible.

Vocals: Bérengère Leroy
Electric guitar: Alain Massoulier
Drums: Stanislas Lepelle
Bass: Sébastien Vaugan
Keyboard: Frédéric Lejeune
Music by: Lejeune/Lepelle
Words by: Pierre Mazart
Produced by: The Holograms and 'JBM'

One girl, four boys. That was the Holograms. Five people from diverse backgrounds who would never otherwise have met, drawn together by music. A middle-class doctor's son: Alain. A provincial girl from Burgundy who dreamt of being a singer and had come to Paris to study at the École du Louvre: Bérengère. A dentist's son from Neuilly, enrolled at the Beaux-Arts but only interested in drums: Stanislas Lepelle. The son of a train driver who played synthesiser and longed to be a songwriter: Frédéric Lejeune. And finally the son of a cobbler from Juvisy with a little shoe-repair and key-cutting shop: Sébastien Vaugan, who could play bass guitar like no one else. Then Pierre Mazart, their lyricist, had arrived. A bit older than them and with no connection to music, he sold objets d'art and was destined to be an antique dealer. Passionate about literature and poetry, he had taken up the challenge of songwriting in English and was responsible for the track that would have been their hit, 'Such Stuff as Dreams Are Made On'. It was a quote from Shakespeare, a mysterious, esoteric quote which fitted the new-wave aura perfectly. Bérengère had met him at a party thrown by students at the École du Louvre, along with his younger brother, Jean-Bernard Mazart, known as JBM.

Stretched out on his bed, Alain was hit by a sudden wave of nostalgia, or perhaps it was despondency, maybe even the beginning of depression. In any case, none of the props of his trade – stethoscope, blood pressure cuff, syrups, pills – would be any use in diagnosing the problem or supplying a remedy.

When the Holograms were around, there had been forty-fives; he would go and buy them at the record shop or at Monoprix. The record shop had been replaced by a grocer whose late opening had seen off the Félix Potin on the street. And that shop had changed hands several times before becoming what it was today, a phone shop selling the latest iPhones and iPads with their apps for downloading music or film.

The photographic shop had also disappeared. You would go there to buy Kodak films with twelve, twenty-four or a maximum of thirty-six exposures, and sometimes when you collected them a week later, half the pictures were fuzzy. Now even the cheapest mobile phone allowed you to take more than three thousand photographs for free, visible immediately and often of extremely high quality. Uttering the phrase 'I'll just take a photo with my phone' would have made you sound like a lunatic thirty-three years ago, thought Alain. Being able to phone anyone you liked in the street was not even a dream in 1983, not even an idea, not even foreseen. *What for?* most people would have replied to the idea of an iPhone.

What remained now of the 1980s? Very little, if anything,

concluded Alain. Television channels had multiplied from six to more than a hundred and fifty according to the satellite subscription he had. Where there used to be just one remote control, now you had to juggle with three (flat-screen TV, DVD player and satellite box). These machines were constantly updating and three-quarters of their buttons remained an unused mystery. Everything was digital now and so sophisticated that it was possible to do almost anything sitting in a café. The web had given unlimited access to everything, absolutely everything: from Harvard courses to porn films, by way of the rarest of songs that previously only a few fanatics scattered across the world would have possessed on vinyl, but which were now available to anybody on YouTube.

The print editions of the Encyclopædia Britannica and its door-to-door salesmen no longer existed – everything was on Wikipedia. The medical dictionary with its horrifying illustrations which had previously been the domain of professionals was now available to absolutely anyone in three clicks. And there were forums where patients played at being trainee doctors. In never-ending discussions sometimes going on for several years. Laymen, with no one to moderate their opinions, exchanged erroneous diagnoses and inappropriate treatments. For a long time now, Alain had had to put up with patients interrupting him with the infamous 'Yes, but, Doctor, I read on the internet ...'

And what of the 'idols' of that era? David Bowie had emerged from his British solitude to launch a final album, *Blackstar*, only to bow out of life two days later. The accompanying video was a carefully orchestrated farewell to his fans. U2's Bono only cared about poverty and about becoming Secretary General of the United Nations – and perhaps that's what he would become one day. Ravaged by plastic surgery, Michael Jackson had finished his life as a quasi-transsexual dependent on sleeping pills right up until the final overdose, with his career overshadowed by sordid rumours of his behaviour with little boys. As for the enigmatic Prince, before he was found dead at his Paisley Park studios, he had only made rare appearances for unexpected secret concerts, and other than that only communicated through the web, making new songs available for download. No one knew if he still had a following who bought them.

Of course there were idols today. Alain knew about Eminem, Adele, Rihanna and Beyoncé, but beyond that ... The few times he had seen them on music channels had convinced him that the vast majority of music produced round the world today oscillated between rap and pop, sometimes a fortuitous blend of the two, and invariably involved videos of young girls dressed like high-class prostitutes, wearing too much make-up and gyrating around gleaming expensive cars. All the songs sounded the same; they were quite stirring, but aimed squarely at fickle adolescents, who would quickly move on and forget them. The Holograms did not have that problem: no one had forgotten them because no one had ever heard of them.

Enthusiastic Beginnings

They would get together to practise at the weekend. Usually in Juvisy, in the garage of Sébastien Vaugan's neat stone villa. Sébastien's father's Peugeot 204 had to be driven out and parked on a little side street first. Vaugan, who had just passed his driving test, took care of that, mostly before the others arrived. At the back of the garage there were lots of tools attached to the wall and there was a wood lathe which the cobbler had used to make his dining-room table and chairs himself. In addition, there was an old Communist Party poster probably dating back to the sixties, which exhorted the workers to unite for the Revolution. Vaugan wouldn't talk about that. His father was a member of the Party, but Vaugan was a reserved young man who never spoke about his personal life apart from bass and records.

Bérengère had encountered Lepelle one afternoon when she was going to meet her boyfriend at the Beaux-Arts. The brass band of the famous college was in full flow in the courtyard and Lepelle was in charge of taking the money. In a break, Lepelle had hurried over to the young girl who was watching the band play and smoking a cigarette.

'What you're listening to is rubbish. I don't care about that poxy band or about taking money. What I'm into is drums. I'd like to join a group, a real group. I want to be a drummer.'

'Like Charlie Watts?' Bérengère had asked him.

'Better than Charlie Watts!' Lepelle had replied. 'He's not that good, Charlie Watts, although I'm glad you mention him; normally when people talk about the Stones they only talk about Mick Jagger or Keith Richards. Are you into music?'

Bérengère had replied that she was a singer. Two months earlier she had discovered a piano-bar in a cellar near Notre-Dame, called L'Acajou. She had gone for an audition and now sang there two nights a week from ten o'clock until midnight. She earned a hundred and fifty francs a night, just pocket money. She sang Barbara, Gainsbourg, a bit of Sylvie Vartan, but what she loved most was Bowie and, more than anything, 'wave'.

Lepelle had gone to L'Acajou one evening and met the pianist. He said he was a bit too old to set up a group, but he knew a lad who was great on keyboards – the son of an old regiment mate by the name of Frédéric. He gave them his phone number. Frédéric Lejeune joined their project. The first three Holograms were therefore keyboards, drums and a singer, and they played at open-air concerts and in little suburban venues.

One evening, Lepelle suddenly said, 'Would you like to go out with me? You're very beautiful, really.'

'Thanks for the "really".'

'I didn't mean it like that. You know what I meant …'

There had been an embarrassed silence, then Lepelle heard her say, 'You're cool, Stanislas, but I don't want to go out with you.'

'OK,' Lepelle said reluctantly, 'well, we're not going to break up the group over this.' He then went on, mendaciously, 'Anyway, I have so many girls after me at the Beaux-Arts, I can't handle them all.'

*

It was decided that they should make the group bigger. They couldn't carry on with just the three of them; they needed a bass player and an electric guitarist. And also they couldn't just go on doing cover versions, they needed to write their own songs. Frédéric Lejeune composed nice tunes, but, according to Lepelle, they lacked ambition. A guitarist and a bassist would bring a new element. The three decided to put an advert in *Rock & Folk*. Ten bassists turned up. Most of them were not nearly good enough, but then Vaugan began to play. When he finished his piece, he looked up and murmured, 'I don't do that very often, it's my first audition.'

'And your last,' Lepelle responded, 'because you're with us now. Don't you agree, Bérengère?'

Then there had been the audition for the guitarist and Alain was chosen. Now the Holograms were five.

Lejeune's melodies improved, Bérengère's voice became more and more assured, Alain perfected his solos whilst studying for second-year medicine, Lepelle neglected the studios of the Beaux-Arts in order to concentrate on his drumming and Vaugan's playing remained excellent even though he was busy with his carpentry training. But the words of their songs still posed a problem. Lepelle had undertaken a first draft of three songs but the words were ridiculous: mysterious girls, nights without end under a red moon, what a boon. Alain had tried to write one too but no one had liked that either. Vaugan refused even to try, as did Lejeune. They had quite liked Bérengère's attempts, but judged them a bit too feminine.

They looked into the cost of hiring a studio but it was exorbitant so they had opted instead to record some songs in the Vaugans' garage. This necessitated stopping mid-song when a moped went by or when the neighbour's dog barked.

The resulting sound was not great, but acceptable for a demo to be sent to a record company. In the end, though, the group decided to wait until they had 'something mind-blowing', to quote Alain, before they sent anything off.

'You're right, man,' Lepelle decided, 'we need a songwriter and a proper studio. And we'll have to sing in English if we want to have worldwide appeal. We're not trying to be Indochine or Téléphone. We want to be better than U2, better than the Eurythmics, better than Depeche Mode. We're the Holograms and we're going to be the best!'

'Les Mots Bleus'

An idea began to form in his mind. An idea that would help to dispel his feelings of fury and injustice. He would contact them. There was no reason why he should be the only one to know that they had actually succeeded in bagging a meeting to discuss songs of which he no longer had a recording. Still in pain, Alain got up and went over to his desk, almost knocking into his examination table, and, sitting down, turned on his computer.

They may not have had a career with the Holograms, but some of them were quite well known. Sébastien Vaugan was easy to track down – the French Billiards Academy, which served as his headquarters, was in the phone book, but Alain wanted if at all possible to avoid asking him anything at all. The plump, shy boy with the genius for playing bass had become an extreme right-wing thug. At fifty-three, muscular, with a shaved head and always dressed in black T-shirt and leather jacket, Vaugan, known simply by his surname, was a rabble-rouser and the head of an extremist group, called the WWP – White Western Party. He'd been all over the internet for years and had been convicted several times for inciting racial hatred, offences against the police and magistrates, and slandering journalists.

This ghost from the past had kept popping up in Alain's life every few years, in the most diverse places. Their paths had last crossed six years ago in a restaurant. Before that it had been in a DIY shop, at a funfair in the Tuileries Gardens, and once by the baggage carousel at Orly. Each time, Vaugan seemed happy to see Alain; each time Alain had promised to have a drink with him, and each time he had failed to follow it up, without Vaugan ever seeming to hold it against him. Alain did not, however, feel that a further meeting, which this time would not be by chance, was really called for.

When the coloured Google logo appeared, Alain typed in 'Stan Lepelle'. Their old drummer had dropped 'Stanislas' and now preferred 'Stan'. He was enjoying increasing fame in the world of contemporary art. Twenty years ago he had attracted attention with an installation of thirty thousand pencil sharpeners and pencils in the Colonnes de Buren. He had stayed there a full week, day and night, sharpening all the pencils right to the end, until all that remained were shavings that his assistants gathered up and his dealer then sold, elegantly set in glass. Alain had taken his family to see the artist, but was told he could not be interrupted. He had bought one of the glass discs containing shavings, though, and it now adorned one of the bedrooms in his holiday home in Noirmoutier.

There were numerous results on the Net for Lepelle. Alain read through his Wikipedia entry which listed all his installations across the globe, giant structures – of a die, a key, a light bulb – in urban or rustic settings, but all creating an unusual effect. Next he clicked on Lepelle's website and saw his official picture: frowning, with very short hair. Over the years he had seen that face several times in various magazines like *Connaissance des arts* or *Art actuel*. The website also listed the numerous prizes awarded to Lepelle's work throughout the world. At the top of the page, the thumbnail marked 'Contact' displayed the email address of a prestigious gallery in Avenue Matignon. Alain wrote it in his notebook.

When he typed in 'Frédéric Lejeune' an impressive number of Frédéric Lejeunes appeared. None of them seemed to be the one he was looking for. In about 2001, Frédéric had sent him a brochure for a hotel he had just opened in Thailand. He had obviously gone through his old diaries and sent a copy of the brochure to all his old contacts. That was how Alain had learnt that the keyboard and synthesiser player from the Holograms had decided to make a new life for himself in Thailand. The last time he had thought of him was on hearing the news of the tsunami. Had Frédéric and his hotel been carried off in the tide of rubbish that the wave had swept into the towns? Out of curiosity he had checked several times on the Net. It seemed that the 'little paradise of relaxation in the Land of Smiles' was still standing. After putting in some key words along with his old friend's name, like 'Thailand', 'resort' or 'little paradise', Alain succeeded in finding the 'Bao Thai Resort', still being described as the 'little paradise of relaxation in the Land of Smiles'.

Next he searched for 'Bérengère Leroy', and again several faces appeared and none of them corresponded to what Bérengère would look like today. Alain quickly gave up. Bérengère was not to be found. Her parents owned a *relais* in Burgundy but he had forgotten the name of it and had never been there; JBM was the only one who had. Anyway, Bérengère would almost certainly be married. When women married, they changed their names and disappeared from listings and directories. Alain had not even bothered to put JBM's name into Google. JBM was so far removed from him now he would never reply.

An hour later, Alain had sent an email to the three contacts jotted down in his notebook: Lejeune in Thailand, Lepelle at his gallery and Pierre Mazart at his antique shop Au Temps Passé on the Left Bank. It was Pierre who had written 'Such Stuff as Dreams Are Made On'. Pierre had always been passionate about the past and history of art, and perhaps he would have kept the cassette and could make him a copy. To thank him, Alain decided he would buy an ornament from his shop. Perhaps a mortar – he had broken the white marble one from his father's day and patients liked seeing old-fashioned medical artefacts in the consulting room. It reassured them about the expertise of their doctor. The prospect of unburdening himself to someone else about the letter was comforting and he felt his backache receding a little.

Before switching off the computer, Alain typed in 'new wave'. About a hundred and thirty-four million results came up. According to Wikipedia, new wave (or 'nouvelle vague' which took its name from the French cinematic movement of the 1950s) was used to describe 'the new, mainly Anglo-American pop-rock groups and artists who followed on from the explosion of punk, incorporating electronic music, experimental music, disco and pop'. Also listed were all the sub-categories of new wave: synthpop, electronic music, New Romantics and cold wave.

That's all rather clinical, thought Alain, for whom new wave and cold wave came together in a subtle fusion that had produced that cold but chic, industrial but luxurious sound. Earlier on, with the Beatles, the Stones or even Led Zeppelin it was easy to recognise the various instruments and there was hardly any difference between the recorded sound and the live sound. Mixing and working up sounds had evolved in less than ten years, led by pioneers like Kraftwerk before coming to full fruition with the Eurythmics. Poetry sung in English accompanied by sophisticated melodies invaded the French music scene in the early eighties. Alain's view was that wave had been heralded several years earlier by one song. A cold, pure, magical song. A crystal of a song lasting three minutes forty-five seconds. Even though there were sometimes disagreements within the group, everyone agreed on that point: the song was genius. To Alain, it was more than genius, it was quite simply the ideal song. All the artistic attempts of Western poetry from Ronsard to Baudelaire were just drafts, just vague, clumsy pieces of research in comparison. Paul Éluard, André Breton and Apollinaire had, in their own modern times, come close to that ideal without quite succeeding. Finally, in the year of our Lord 1974, the singer and composer Daniel Bevilacqua, known as Christophe, aided by the young author Jean-Michel Jarre, succeeded in describing love and the paralysing impossibility of expressing it fully to the object of your affections. They had written 'Les Mots Bleus'.

Alain had discovered it in that halcyon period between fifteen and twenty-one, the only time of life when you are truly capable of experiencing love. There is, for that brief period, an openness of mind and body which never returns again. Life will ensure that your brain and your time are taken over by other commitments: preparation for exams, worries about the future, then your career, courses, salary, money, paperwork, etc. The interlude arrives much too early in life, at an age when, apart from some overachievers, experts in flirting and sex, no one is ready.

Alain well remembered his adolescent self in his parents' apartment, hanging out in the bedroom that would later become his son's. He lay on the bed listening to the high-pitched, tragic voice of Christophe telling the remarkable story of the girl coming out of the *mairie* and of the boy who wanted to talk to her. The hypnotic music and the reverberation of the singer's voice, as if he were declaiming couplets in a Romanesque church, took him to vertiginous highs that no drug could have given him. 'Les Mots Bleus' addressed itself to another part of his brain, touched his sensibility in an incredible way that brought tears to his eyes. The second part that began:

> *Il n'y a plus d'horloge, plus de clocher*
> *Dans le square les arbres sont couchés*
> *Je reviens par le train de nuit*
> *Sur le quai je la vois*
> *Qui me sourit*
> *Il faudra bien qu'elle comprenne*
> *À tout prix*

was almost too much to bear. He pictured himself on an empty platform at Gare de Lyon on a warm summer evening. He was getting off a train carrying a heavy travel bag. Bérengère came towards him in slow motion, then threw herself into his arms. He felt her body against his, the softness of her neck, the smell of her hair, then found her mouth, and her tongue excited by the desire of their reunion. In this sequence worthy of a David Lean film, of which he would have been the producer, the director and the only member of the audience, there could be no doubt: she was his girlfriend. Carried away by the lacerating music and his mental images, he could not stop himself from sobbing at the end of the song. It was magical. It was an infinite pain that he had never felt before. That he would never feel again.

He had been nineteen and Bérengère was not his girlfriend,

but the girlfriend of a boy a little older than they were, who was already earning a lot of money. He was the one who paid for the recording of five songs in an upmarket studio that he rented complete with two sound engineers. At twenty-three he had already succeeded in life. He was the brother of their lyricist; he had a melancholic expression and a cat-like smile. He was already known just by his initials: JBM.

The Man with the Cat-like Smile

The black Lincoln wove silently through the dark empty streets. The phone in Aurore's pocket had been buzzing for the past half-hour with a stream of new texts and voicemails.

'You were right, I shouldn't have gone,' remarked JBM, continuing to stare out of the window at the buildings flashing past.

Aurore, his assistant, said nothing. The driver changed down a gear and the Lincoln entered the Louvre tunnel. Around the tunnel's exit, by the gilded statue of Joan of Arc on Place des Pyramides, is where the ranks of the extreme right gather on 1 May each year. As JBM gazed out at the lights of the tunnel, the staff of *Le Parisien* were writing tomorrow's front-page headline – 'Could he be the one?' – while *Libé* was toying with 'Did someone say Mazart?' Meanwhile *L'Express* had just made the decision to change its cover, sending half the newsroom reaching for Berocca tablets, and opted for 'Will that really do for tonight?' Treading more cautiously, but not wishing to be left out, *Le Figaro* had cleverly thrown together a profile piece provisionally entitled 'So who is Jean-Bernard Mazart?'

François Larnier, who had won his party's backing to stand for president at the primaries and was lined up to appear on the France Télévisions show *The Big Debate*, had come up with the idea that inviting JBM along might add an extra dimension to the panel, and his communications advisers agreed. An invitation had gone out to the economist and businessman several weeks before. In spite of Aurore's reservations, JBM had eventually agreed to take part. They were a good half-hour into the broadcast when JBM came on set, greeted by warm smiles from the official candidate and his team. The programme's presenters gave a brief round-up of his career to date: he had graduated in economics, studied at MIT, had pioneered investment in internet start-ups and was now at the helm of Arcadia, one of the top ten French groups listed in the CAC 40 index with a portfolio of forty-five companies worldwide, mostly in the sphere of software development and firewalls, along with interests in hundreds of web feeds.

JBM had the gift of incredible economic foresight. He had predicted the sub-prime mortgage crisis three months ahead of the crash in an interview that had gone almost unnoticed at the time. He had also anticipated the burst of the dot-com bubble and, even more brilliantly, had invested massively in its predecessor, the Minitel, at a time when users saw it as a gimmick. His detractors dismissed him as a simplistic economist, but JBM would always reply, 'I'm not an economist; I studied economics. It's a different thing.' He claimed it all came down to common sense: however complex a market was, it would always come back to the age-old question of supply and demand, of a person with something to sell and another who may or may not wish to buy it.

Journalists loved him because the clear examples he gave allowed them to write articles their readers would understand. The impending sub-prime crisis was summed up as follows: 'It's like trying to fit an elephant inside your flat. The doors and walls are going to be an issue, so you can widen the doors and knock down the partitions, but that won't solve the underlying problem. The problem is the floor – it's going to collapse under the weight of the elephant, taking the animal, you, and probably the floors below and all your neighbours with it. At the moment, the analysts are only seeing the problem in terms of doors and walls – I see the floor. They see only the volume of the animal – I see its weight.' JBM had put smiles on many newspaper editors' faces with his tale of elephants and weak floors. 'JBM's talking in nursery rhymes for kids, Dumbo before he found his magic feather,' jeered a well-known financial commentator. 'Web visionary he may have been, but his economic analysis leaves much to be desired.' A satirical weekly magazine even depicted JBM as a ringmaster holding a hoop in the shape of France, waiting for an elephant to jump through it. A month later, the economics journalists had stopped laughing, and the mere mention of JBM's name had the effect of a drop of vinegar falling on an oyster. JBM had also made a name for himself by upgrading the operating system used by the military in only two months – rather than the three years projected by the government. The bug-ridden Louvois system, which had never managed to pay soldiers the correct amount, became a political hot potato as soon as it was replaced by the Arcadia creation Vauban, which never failed to make a payment.

On the TV set, when JBM began to explain in simple terms two possible ways out of the crisis, everybody understood him – a rare occurrence in political debate. When he went on to discuss the French national debt and future employment opportunities linked to the new web economy, everyone understood that, too, and the reporters in the studio exchanged glances. JBM had gone more than a minute over his allotted time and everyone had forgotten all about the official candidate – his adviser was throwing panicked looks at the presenter, who was pretending not to notice. It was JBM in the hot seat, and he had an answer to every question: businesses going under, the influence of Brussels on French policy, working hours, pensions ... On social networks, mentions of 'JBM – Jean-Bernard Mazart' were mounting up by the minute. Interns who had been told to keep half an eye on the 'likes', 'comments' and 'shares' on the programme's website and Facebook wondered if there was a bug on their server, the notifications were coming in so quickly. Over the past fifteen minutes the programme had reached a 30 per cent audience share. Three minutes later, it became the most watched programme of the night across all channels.

Eventually BFM-TV's Jean-Jacques Bourdin, looking like an ageing rock star, stepped in before his colleagues had a chance to speak, aware that he was taking his place in TV history – perhaps even in the history of France itself. 'One last question and it's a straightforward one. We're six months away from the next presidential election. Why not throw your hat in the ring?'

Aurore jumped. Bourdin caught her eye for a split second and she gave him the hardest stare she could muster, trying to convey that she would knock his chair over and scratch his face until she drew blood if she could. Slightly thrown, JBM raised his eyebrows and smiled.

'Your assistant's frowning,' the journalist teased.

The camera swung round to Aurore, whose expression was now impassive.

'Come on then, what do you say?' Bourdin pressed him.

The room went silent. JBM glanced round at the official candidate, who had by now realised the extent to which he had shot himself in the foot by inviting the Arcadia boss to share the stage with him, and glared back at him. JBM understood the meaning of the look, but all he could do was to keep smiling.

'No, honestly, I don't think so,' he said at last.

'Really?' Jean-Jacques Bourdin asked coolly.

The switchboard was abuzz and tweets were streaming in at two hundred a second.

'Are you sure?' The journalist pressed JBM for an answer as his colleagues seethed, ready to see him castrated on live TV for having dared to steal their scoop.

'OK,' JBM wrapped things up. 'I think that'll do for tonight.'

He stood up and shook hands with the journalists before taking the cold, sticky hand of the official presidential hopeful, who watched him walk out of the studio and told himself that the man would be the death of him. That, as his life drew to a close, he would see JBM's tall, slim frame and silver hair silhouetted under the spotlights.

The Lincoln pulled up on the gravel driveway. Max, the driver, opened the door to let JBM and Aurore out and they walked up the front steps. The sound of the television could be heard coming from the living room. On the flat-screen TV, François Larnier was trying to speak convincingly about his plans for tackling youth unemployment. He listed his proposals on his fingers like a child counting, while knitting his brow, apparently aiming to more closely resemble a grown man. Blanche lowered the volume and clapped slowly, without looking round at her husband.

'You're the next president of this country,' she said. 'And I know what I'm talking about. My father did too. Domitile Kavanski called,' she added breezily, picking up a petit four from the tray beside her.

'Who?'

Blanche turned in her white leather armchair, smiling in simultaneous disdain and despair.

'Domitile Kavanski,' she repeated more loudly.

The name, which began softly and ended like the crack of a whip, did not bode well. JBM and Aurore exchanged looks.

'Don't tell me she didn't get hold of you, Aurore?'

'She did,' replied Aurore. 'She sent me five texts.'

'And you didn't say anything?' gasped Blanche.

'I was waiting for the right moment. She's the number one publicist in France,' she said, turning to JBM.

'Call her back straight away,' Blanche told her.

'Out of the question,' JBM shot back.

'I'll leave you to it ...'

'No, don't go, Aurore,' JBM replied. 'Do you want to stay here?'

'I'm going home, JBM.'

'Fine. I'll show Aurore out.'

'Now Blanche is on my back – that's the last thing I need,' grumbled JBM as they walked along the covered walkway that led to the garden.

'Yep, good luck with that,' Aurore replied evenly.

Max got out of the car and opened the door. As Aurore was about to walk down the steps, JBM took her by the arm and held her back.

'Listen, tell me. What should we do?'

When things got hectic, he sometimes forgot to use the polite *vous* form of address. This was not true of Aurore, who bit her lip, paused and said, 'You play the game. A bit of PR with Kavanski will get Blanche off your case. You already have a profile; you'll become even better known, and if the wave starts to rise you stand aside and let it keep coming, and then ...'

'And then?'

'You use an interview as the opportunity to make a smooth exit, like Jacques Delors quashing rumours of presidential aspirations on *7 sur 7* in 1994. And there you have it, joke over.'

'And there you have it ... You might be on to something, you know.'

'You run with the hare and hunt with the hounds, then you leave the hare be and take the hounds back to their kennels, end of story.'

'I don't know what I'd do without you,' he said.

Aurore smiled and shrugged, and headed towards the car.

'How old were you in 1994?' JBM called after her.

'Eleven, I think!' replied Aurore.

The driver closed the car door after her with a dull thud, the headlights came on and they drove off down the gravel drive. JBM returned to the house.

'You're all they're talking about!' Blanche called from the living room.

JBM veered off into the kitchen and poured himself a glass of Chablis.

Blanche

The Lincoln and its driver are more or less the only luxuries JBM allows himself; the only property he owns is an 180 m^2 flat in Paris that he's never lived in and has rented out for years. That flat, three paperweights and a collection of old telephone directories aside, all his possessions would fit inside one suitcase. He finds the idea of paying seventy-five thousand euros for a return flight to New York in a Fan Jet Falcon ridiculous and unnecessary; he's always used commercial airlines. 'You're a kind of ascetic,' I've often told him. 'You turned up here with your suitcase and your books, and you've no more to show for yourself twenty-eight years on. All you've got is a new Lincoln and a new driver when the old one retired. Oh, wait, and a watch ...' I think that really is the only thing I've known him treat himself to – a Breguet, the kind of watch that lasts a lifetime, so he'll never buy another one. I don't think I've ever truly understood the man – he was made to live alone, with a computer, a bottle of water and a driver. You could leave him like that for months and he'd be absolutely fine. He avoids socialising with the rich, never accepts gifts, does his best to get out of invitations. People sense this about him before they even meet him, this kind of reserve. They find him mysterious. There's no mystery to him; my husband is the only businessman in France who'd eat a plate of egg mayonnaise and a bottle of Perrier at a bistro counter for lunch – and he does it, quite often. He never has any money on him; it's unheard of for him to have two hundred euros in his wallet. I actually don't think he likes money.

When I met him, he was living in the junior suite of a hotel – not your average neighbourhood guesthouse, but not a five-star palace either. I was fascinated by him – a man without possessions, no flat, no house, no paintings. Nothing, except an American car and the services of a driver to take him around France and Europe. His suitcase was always left out; he didn't even bother putting it away in the wardrobe. It was as if he might be leaving at the end of the day, or within the hour. I asked him how long exactly he had been living there. He took his time before answering, 'Three years, I think ... maybe four. I forget.' 'Why here?' 'I had lunch here once ...' he said, as if the fact you had once eaten at a hotel could explain the fact you were living there all year round, four years later. Suite 418. When I got home to my own place, everyone around me seemed puffed up, pretentious, totally frivolous. I couldn't stop thinking about him, back in suite 418. When he bought his flat, he found it difficult to feel at home there; it felt too big. He decided to rent it out and go back to his hotel room. After that, everything happened very quickly.

My parents both died in the same year, five months apart. I can't describe how hard and how wrong it feels to have to share your grief with the press. It was all they talked about: the magazines ran front-page stories about 'Heiress Blanche de Caténac', along with pictures of me in dark glasses. I can't help having a corneal defect that means I'm sensitive to bright lights. This Hollywood-style accessory must have given me an air of mystery, and they played it up to the max. The magazines kept up their soap opera, projecting fantasies from American

TV series onto me, tarring me with the brush of 1980s popular culture – *Dallas*, *Dynasty* and so on – the way they tarred and feathered people to punish them in Westerns. All of the Caténac group's holdings were splashed across the papers: luxury hotels, casinos, restaurants. At least they only saw the tip of the iceberg; they knew nothing about the company's interests abroad, the other hotel chains or spas, still less the office spaces rented out all over the world. JBM was there, by my side. Just by being there, he reassured me. That's something the journalists have never said, but JBM is a reassuring person; his calmness and his smile are more effective than any over-the-counter remedy. When he's around, you're not afraid of anything, because he's not afraid. He's never afraid. I can't say he helped me take control of the group – my father had long since told me everything I needed to know, and the two faithful advisers who had worked with him for more than twenty-five years were there to support me.

The mansion and surrounding gardens right in the middle of Paris were now mine. 'Don't go back to your hotel. Come to my place,' I said. 'Come to our place.' I remember very clearly saying those words: 'Come to our place.' And we got married and had children, and this time JBM put his suitcase away in the back of the wardrobe. I remember he was on a work trip once, and I took out the suitcase and asked the housekeeper to throw it away. I did it so he could never use it again, never leave again. One day he said, 'Hang on, that's odd. Where's my suitcase? I could have sworn I put it in there.' I shrugged and mumbled that I had no idea.

I think part of the reason I loved JBM was that my parents loved him, especially my father; he didn't really understand what JBM did – still less this 'net' thing he was predicting would be big – but he was impressed by his success. It wasn't every day you came across a young man of twenty-six who had already made two million francs. We kept his investments in Minitel Rose sex chatlines well hidden from my mother. She would have preferred me to go out with the heir to an empire like ours. JBM comes from a comfortable background – his father was a lawyer, his mother an interior designer – but not on the scale of the Caténacs. As an only child, I was mollycoddled, always well turned out; I went to the most exclusive places and even took part in one of those hideous debutantes' balls.

When the coming of the internet took place as he had prophesied, Arcadia, the company he had founded and which had become one of the major players in new technologies, took on the digitisation of the Caténac group. It was the first time I'd heard the word 'digitisation'. Other than him, nobody used it. JBM came with me to a board meeting and read out a ten-point plan headed 'Second World'. In it, he described the real world as we all knew it and in which the group had thus far been operating, and another world that was just around the corner: a 'mirror' world made up of virtual transactions, but real customers. The board members listened, feeling something between astonishment and fascination. He was predicting that hotels could be booked online, not via agencies but by customers themselves, sitting at their computers on the other side of the world, and that 'platforms', which were not yet called websites, would be created on which gamblers could play through the networks using their bank cards. He said we had to be the first to board the train, that it would never pass through again. I can still hear him now, pausing in his presentation to look the board members in the eye: 'There will be no second chance; don't even let that thought cross your mind. This isn't a logistical evolution, but a complete change of paradigm. Those who don't get on this train will be left behind in the old world. They'll die, and they won't go gently ... They'll be annihilated.'

I supported him, and the board members voted through his three-year plan by a slim majority. The years that followed bore out his ten points. When our competitors began to panic at the rise of the Net, we had already been operational for over two years. Whereas others were starting from scratch, we were improving on what we had already built. Many years later, JBM approached Kodak, wanting to buy a stake in the company, and advising them to make the shift into digital images, freeing up two hundred million dollars of their own funds to buy up all the patents in new gel-image technology, which he saw as the future of the camera industry. The firm refused, perceiving his offer as a takeover bid. 'They can't see that I'm trying to save them,' he said often over the course of those months. Less than a year later, the Kodak empire, which had dominated global photographic and cinematographic film production for almost a century, declared itself bankrupt and practically disappeared.

JBM has made millions for the Caténac group – hundreds of millions. My husband is a genius. My husband is the kind of man plenty of women dream of. He's given me two bright sons. Everything's good, everything's perfect. But have I ever loved him? Am I even capable of loving anyone? Since the day I was born, my life has been made up of codes, labels, money, connections. Not love. I've never known frivolity or insouciance. I don't think JBM has either. I've often told myself that's the main thing we have in common. But he has been capable of loving, I'm sure of it. There are two people he has loved: his brother, his eccentric brother with his encyclopedic knowledge, his objets d'art, his auctions and his decadent dandy ways. His brother, yes, and Aurore, his assistant. His inseparable Aurore Delfer. I think if JBM was to do one of those lists he's so good at, entitled 'What would you take with you to a desert island?', Pierre Mazart's porphyry urn and Aurore would be near the top of the list. I would come after. That's if he remembered to mention me at all.

675 x 564

Aurore opened her bag in the car and took out the latest issue of *Forbes*. The magazine had been delivered to her by courier that afternoon and she had not yet had a chance to read it. She kept turning the pages until she reached the article she was looking for: 'Tycoon's Angels'. An insight into the lives of personal assistants. 'They're young, they're beautiful, they live in the shadow of the most powerful men in finance and they know secrets they will never tell,' the article began in the glamour-loving style the glitzy magazine was known for. Interviews with six assistants from six different countries followed, accompanied by a photo of each woman with her boss.

'To find out more about this unique and fascinating career,' the journalist gushed, 'we talk to six women in the business. From the United States to Japan, by way of France and Russia, the role of business PA involves organising meetings and business trips, drafting correspondence, preparing files, undertaking research and helping with decision-making. Business person and PA must understand one another perfectly. At this level of responsibility, the boundaries between professional and private lives are blurred. The word "personal" appears in "personal assistant" and makes all the difference, because working so closely together can make these roles very psychologically and emotionally demanding. "It's important to remember it's just a job!" explains Jenny Davis (page 55). The role requires many of the same skills as an executive assistant, with particular weight put on language skills, given the number of contacts PAs have to deal with abroad. One of the most rewarding aspects of the job can be having your opinion taken on board by a high-ranking business person, and sometimes even changing their mind. The personal assistant is an essential link, and all the business person's contacts know her. She is the last line of defence before gaining direct access to her boss, "the invisible fortress", as Aurore Delfer puts it (see interview page 57).'

Aurore flicked on two pages to find her interview and photo, taken a year earlier after a conference in London. With her phone wedged between her shoulder and ear, she had one hand pointing towards a photographer and the other resting on JBM's shoulder while he looked on. 'More than a bodyguard!' read the caption. 'Aurore Delfer, personal assistant of French economist and businessman Jean-Bernard Mazart, also known as JBM. Probably the most discreet of the women we interviewed, but one of the most powerful. Former assistant to the Secretary-General of the European Commission, she left her job to work for JBM seven years ago, becoming, at the age of twenty-six, the youngest assistant ever to work for such a prominent figure. JBM and Aurore are undoubtedly one of the most endearing of our duos.' Aurore was reminded of those magazine features in which celebrities were asked to talk about and pose with their pets. She skimmed over the terse answers to the interview she had already read and signed off a month before.

Forbes: You're the youngest of our six assistants at this level of responsibility ...

Aurore: I started out very young and I'm grateful for the opportunities I've been given.

Forbes: Has anyone tried to headhunt you?

Aurore: I've had some offers.

Forbes: But you haven't followed up on them?

Aurore: Obviously not.

Forbes: Your nickname is 'the invisible fortress'. Does that bother you?

Aurore: I'm used to it. If you think about it, it's quite a fitting metaphor for our profession, or part of it, at least. It's to do with his phone: other than his friends and family and a few close contacts, nobody has JBM's mobile number; they have to go through me.

Forbes: In French, there are two forms of address: *vous* and, less formally, *tu*. Do you call each other *tu*?

Aurore: No, we use *vous*. I don't think we could ever switch to *tu*. It works well as it is.

Forbes: How did you meet JBM?

Aurore: Seven years ago, I was one of the assistants to Mario Moncelli [*Editor's note*: Secretary-General of the European Commission]. JBM was at the European Parliament for a digital conference. I went up to him at the drinks reception and told him I'd like to work for him.

Forbes: Not shy, are you!

Aurore: No, I'm not.

Forbes: Why were you so keen to work with him?

Aurore: He asked me exactly the same question. He didn't wait for my answer, but asked me what 675 times 564 makes.

Forbes: And?

Aurore: And the answer is 380,700. He was very surprised I knew the answer, and asked me to do some other calculations. I got them all right. Both of us happen to be able to do complex sums in our heads. That immediately gave us something in common. I left Mario Moncelli's staff and started at Arcadia as second assistant. Six months later, JBM's assistant decided on a career change – as happens quite often in our line of work – and JBM asked me to work directly alongside him.

Aurore opened the door of her flat. Inside there was no husband, children, dog or cat. Nothing, not even a lover any more. The last one had found it difficult to put up with a girlfriend who was away half the time and earned five times his salary. She looked at herself in the mirror in the hall and saw a pretty young woman with very long blonde hair and eyes that were still sharp in spite of her tiredness. Her phone gave a little buzz.

JBM
Goodnight Aurore, thanks for existing.

Revamp

'Who is JBM?' asked the front page of *Le Figaro* above a photo of the businessman. He had grey hair now, almost white at the temples, but still the same slightly melancholy expression, the same cat-like smile. His hands were clasped in front of him and you could see the domed blue cufflinks. The photo must have been taken at a conference. He looked as if he were listening attentively to something or someone. *Le Figaro* didn't mention anything about JBM that was not already familiar to Alain. And the one thing the journalist did not say was that in 1983 JBM had financed the new-wave group the Holograms.

The night before, Alain and Véronique had watched the programme eating *croque-monsieurs*. It was François Larnier's face that stayed in Alain's memory. The camera had not missed his fleeting expression of total panic. The unfortunate man must have felt the ground giving way under his feet. JBM had buried him without making the slightest effort, like those people who crush their pets when reversing into the garage of their second home. They hear a loud squealing, then nothing. 'We've killed Médor.' The official candidate had not even squealed. He had let himself be squashed in silence – totally squashed in fact. 'Isn't he the one who went out with your singer?' Véronique had asked. Alain had muttered, 'Yes, it was him.'

*

That morning Alain's back was a little better.

'I've contacted the others,' he said, folding up the newspaper. He said it in the same matter-of-fact tone he would say, 'I'm going to put you on antibiotics.'

'There has to be someone who still has a copy of the cassette,' he went on, seeking Véronique's approval and also trying to convince himself he had done the right thing.

Véronique, who had already emerged from the bathroom, impeccably coiffed and dressed, nodded. 'That's good; that will keep you occupied. So who will you go and see first? Your friend Vaugan?'

Alain noticed her slightly ironic tone. 'No, of course not,' he replied, annoyed. 'I've sent an email to Frédéric Lejeune, but he's in Thailand ...'

Véronique raised her eyebrows with a little pursing of the lips that seemed to indicate that was an illogical thing to have done.

'And I've sent another to Stan Lepelle, via his gallery, and also one to Pierre Mazart, JBM's brother. He's an antique dealer.'

'Whereabouts?'

'In Paris.'

'Why send an email? He has a shop with opening hours – why not go and see him? It would be a reason for you to go out; you haven't left the flat all week. Get dressed, brush your hair, shave. You can't stay in pyjamas all your life.'

Alain did not reply. Instead he stood up to make himself another Nespresso, reflecting that Véronique was being rather sharp this morning.

*

While he had been in bed, he'd had the impression that as his condition deteriorated, Véronique, conversely, was rising earlier and earlier, and that she seemed to be more animated and energetic than she had been for several months. One afternoon he wondered if she had a lover, without being able to think of anyone they knew who could have fulfilled such a role. It was no doubt rather convenient for some husbands tired of their wives to abandon them to the arms of others. The wives would return from their escapades perked up and elegant and much more agreeable to live with. The lover only saw the good side of the spouse. The day-to-day irritations and chores, all the things that progressively extinguish love, did not feature in their little interludes during which they were able to lay aside the burdens of life, taking them up again afterwards. Alain had himself considered perhaps taking a mistress. He had reviewed the women of his acquaintance who might agree to an affair with him. The candidates could be counted on the fingers of one hand and were not exactly appetising. Instead of pleasing sensuality, Alain foresaw problems. He had let the idea drop.

Now that he was on his own in the flat, he picked up the phone and dialled the number of Au Temps Passé, Pierre's antique shop. After several rings, the answer machine clicked in and Pierre's voice announced the opening hours of the shop, adding that the machine did not accept messages. Véronique was right, all he had to do was go there and the outing would do him good. Alain began to get ready. In the bathroom he removed his bathrobe, grimacing, and looked in the cabinet mirror. He looked rough – he hadn't shaved for a week, and the resulting beard, noticeably white about the chin, in conjunction with his glasses, definitely made him look like his father. Alain reached for the shaving foam and a razor. Half an hour later, he was impeccably shaven, and had even trimmed his hair a little with scissors borrowed from Véronique. He had also found a box of contact lenses still within their expiry date. The rimless glasses that were supposedly 'as good as a facelift' were consigned to the bathroom bin along with Véronique's make-up removal pads. Before dropping them in, Alain had given them a vicious twist, though not without a thought for the pitiful sum his insurance company had reimbursed him for their purchase.

Now the mirror told him not that he looked like the Alain of the Holograms, but that he looked like someone who might once have been that Alain. From the wardrobe he chose a black suit and white shirt, then hesitated over a pair of red socks purchased in Rome from a shop that advertised itself as supplying the Vatican and the Pope himself. But he thought better of them and opted instead for a black pair with loafers. The outfit was chic, but simple. In the hallway his eye fell on a walking stick in amongst the umbrellas. The object, which he'd known all his life and must date back to his grandfather, was not without elegance, but was reminiscent either of a dandy, which wasn't an appropriate look for a doctor, or old age or illness. Alain put it back with the umbrellas and swallowed two Ibuprofen with a glass of water.

Véronique

Yes, I'm cheating on him. He asked me last night while I was cleaning my teeth; he'd probably been mulling it over since the early afternoon. I looked at him in his pyjamas in the mirror and I felt like laughing – but I didn't. I felt like saying, 'Yes, I'm cheating on you – so what?' just to see the look on his face – but I didn't do that either. I just rolled my eyes, rinsed my mouth out and said irritably, 'What kind of a question is that? Anything else you'd like to ask?' Alain dropped it straight away and went to lie down with his hot-water bottle. It doesn't take a lot to make people happy – usually they'll settle for hearing what they want to hear. As soon as they've got their answer, they move on to something else. I'm cheating on him because I'm bored, because after twenty-five years of marriage and two well-brought-up children (which is more than can be said for most), I still feel alive. I'm cheating on him because I wasn't always Dr Massoulier's wife. If he's become obsessed with trying to get back this demo tape from his youth – which, by the way, I find utterly pathetic – well, he's not the only one who remembers being young. Having lovers, having men find me attractive, being taken home at the end of the night, leaving some of my dates at the door and taking others upstairs. I remember getting on planes to meet guys in Italy and Switzerland. I remember the same men – and others – taking planes and trains to come and see me in return.

I don't regret marrying Alain; it was the right time for both of us. Afterwards, I went into a long hibernation. It was an easy life; the kids grew up without too many problems – a few academic setbacks, adolescent crises and the odd falling-out during their school years, but nothing remotely out of the ordinary. We never had to deal with our children taking drugs or falling in with the wrong crowd and having to be picked up from the police station in the middle of the night. As for my career, for a long time it trundled along nicely and brought in a comfortable salary at the end of the month. I looked after five luxury retailers in Paris, designing different window displays for every season. Christmas was, of course, the busiest time. In recent years, business has gradually dwindled, and I've begun to work with mid-range brands and shops alongside my luxury clients. The Chinese have entered the fray, offering a similar service for half the price. Nowadays I only have two very loyal clients and, though I pretend otherwise to Alain, I know full well that sooner or later my business will go down the pan and younger, more dynamic visual merchandisers will come along with snazzy set-ups and props that will take over the market. Alain will never have to face these kinds of problems; he can always rely on the cycle of stomach bugs, hay fever, rhinitis and bronchitis to keep the wheels turning. People will always be ill. In three or four years my business will fold, but I'm not going to throw my hands up in despair – it's out of my control. I've done my best, but there'll be a time when it has to end. However long your winning streak continues, you'll always lose some day and have to leave the table. And I also know that as I enter my late fifties, men's eyes will, shall we say, dwell on me far less.

The first time I thought about cheating on Alain ... No, that's not quite it; it wasn't as clear-cut as that. What happened was that we were at our friends' for drinks one evening and I looked at him. He was talking to the other guests, sitting on the sofa with a glass of whisky in his hand, and I was watching him. It must have been ten years into our marriage. I asked myself if I would have fallen in love with that man if I had met him for the first time there, that evening. If he would have won me over. The answer was no. I'd have found him pleasant, cheerful, certainly, but there was no way I'd have imagined making love to him after the party, still less marrying him and having his children. What makes us fall in love with someone at a given moment? Does what's true of that moment hold true for ever? I'm sure plenty of other wives have looked at their husbands in the same way at some point; who knows what conclusions they've drawn – I don't have very many female friends and it's not something I'd discuss with them. Alain caught me looking at him, raised his eyebrows and asked, 'Everything OK?' Yes, I said, everything was fine. But it wasn't.

After that, I fell back into my state of slumber, waking up a few years later in the arms of one of my clients, who was also married. I used to meet him at a hotel in the middle of the afternoon. We were forty-two and we knew neither of us was planning a divorce – we were just there for a few hours of secret pleasure. We had it all worked out – where I had been and who I had met and the brief summary I would give of my day at the dinner table, and he too must have prepared what to say about the meeting he had supposedly been to, and described it at the table as matter-of-factly as I did. It was easy. Surprisingly so, and I didn't feel guilty about it; perhaps I would have done if I'd had to lie at length, make a convincing argument, come up with a variety of ruses, call on a third person in order to back me up – but no, there was none of that. Come the evening, Alain would utter a few words and the matter was closed. 'How were your clients today, then?' 'It all went well; they were very happy,' and that was that. This had the effect of making my rendezvous at the hotel seem totally unreal. When images from the afternoon came back to me like scenes from a porn film as I made the dinner, it was as if they were from a dream. None of it could really have happened because I was there in the kitchen, keeping an eye on an omelette while my husband watched TV and my children squabbled. The affair went on for a few years and then it came to an end. I fell asleep again.

There have been other awakenings, some better or longer-lasting than others. Then, last week, I realised I would be fifty-eight in five years. And that it was apparent I had caught the eye of a thirty-eight-year-old salesman who had just turned up for the third time to tell me about his teak shelving, specially designed for shop windows. So I ordered some, shut my office door, and asked, 'What are you doing for the next hour?' He replied, 'Nothing.' He smiled, and so did I. And when we kissed, I felt totally alive.

Thyristors and TRIACs

If he had to go back to the start, to where the story began and everything that would later happen was set in motion, JBM would return to an afternoon when he was thirteen and walking back to school with his brother. Sometimes they didn't eat in the school canteen but at home, which was only four bus stops from the lycée. After lunch with their mother, and sometimes an uncle or cousin who happened to be in Paris, they would return to school on the dot of quarter to two. After getting off at the closest bus stop, they had to cross the boulevard and take a side road before arriving at a junction from which they could look across at the tall pale stone façade and the students congregating outside, chatting and smoking in little groups.

Pierre was seventeen, four years older than Jean-Bernard, who was not yet known as JBM. The age difference between the two brothers, which at fifty would seem like nothing at all, felt at the time like a chasm of canyonesque proportions. Pierre was tall, very tall, and already on the large side. He shaved every morning using a brush, shaving soap, and a double-bladed razor with a steel handle that had belonged to their grandfather. He would insert proper bendy razor blades made of bluish steel and screw them in with a little plate to hold them flush against the razor head. JBM didn't shave and still had the smooth skin of a child. Only his melancholy eyes revealed something else in him, something beyond age, beyond any notion of maturity or even masculinity to come; they simply appeared to belong to another person. To a very old soul, returning for one last incarnation. A soul who viewed the world with compassion but feared nothing, having seen it all before.

There was no melancholy in Pierre's eyes; on the contrary, they were constantly alert, always on the lookout. They were the only things he kept right up to the end, those pupils darting about like a bird's. Many years later, Pierre would let his beard grow and become grey and then white at the chin. He would put on thirty kilos and, with his floppy hair swept back, his colourful waistcoats and half-moon spectacles, look like an elderly gent. At the age of fifty, puffing away on a cigar and stroking his beard with fingers laden with gold Roman signet rings, he looked fifteen years older. Hearing him talk, mid-puff, about Ingres, Corot or the marquetry of André-Charles Boulle only added to the strange sense that you were listening to a man who belonged to another time. Pierre had always had a good memory for stories about the great figures of the past, the history of France or local points of interest, and slipped them into conversation so naturally that it was as if he, Pierre Mazart, had seen it all happen himself, just last week.

Cultured beyond his years from a young age, Pierre soon caught the eye of the old antique dealers and collectors, who entrusted him with the role of broker at auctions and markets: he would buy the objects dealers were looking for and sell them to them at a profit, so that they in turn could sell them on to their clients at an even greater profit. Pierre made a decent living from brokering for twelve years before taking over one of his client's shops along with the flat above it, renaming it Au

Temps Passé and finally living his dream of spending his days surrounded by the relics of yesteryear and occasionally agreeing to part with them for a fee. At the height of his glory days, he took part in the Biennale des Antiquaires on several occasions. Pierre married a museum curator, had a son and lived happily for fifteen years until the day his wife decided to drive to their country house in the Auvergne, while Pierre stayed behind to man the shop for the Carré Rive Gauche antiques week. She lost control of the car on a steep B-road, and she and her son were killed. Pierre never remarried, never rebuilt his life, and retreated further into his old books and remnants of the past. During the last years of his life, it was not uncommon to see him wandering around the shop in his dressing gown in the middle of the afternoon, a cigar in his hand, repositioning a crystal chandelier or moving a spotlight whose glare was not to his liking. 'Eccentric' was a word often used to describe him.

Then the economic crisis came and Pierre looked on as a succession of his eldest clients died and the eighteenth- and nineteenth-century art that made up the bulk of his stock went out of favour. He saw the younger generations turn their noses up in distaste at the Louis XV rosewood display cabinets, Napoleonic-era secretaire desks, oil paintings in the style of Claude Gellée and portraits of old aristos in powdered wigs. Those with a vaguely artistic bent and a degree of purchasing power had eyes only for 1950s design: industrial lamps, desks, stools and chairs. Furniture from canteens and architects' offices with which to deck out their living spaces. An artist of limited imagination like Jean Prouvé was now top dog; Prouvé's Trapeze table, made of folded sheet steel in 1956 for the Antony campus student canteen, was auctioned for €1,241,300, including commission. Pierre began to cheer himself up with the odd glass of cognac. Then Jeff Koons's *Balloon Dog* was sold at Christie's for $58.4 million. For weeks afterwards, Pierre went round telling anyone who would listen that the world had gone mad, it was only a metal dog that looked like it was made of balloons, a decoration fit for a funfair. The glasses of cognac began mounting up until Pierre was drinking a bottle a day, sometimes two. It reached the point where he occasionally lay down on a Louis XV day bed in the shop and slept until lunchtime. His brother would come and see him but Pierre would never listen; the words 'nervous breakdown' and 'detox' went in one ear and out of the other.

If Pierre were to be believed, the French were not only indifferent to their own country's history and culture, they had no interest in the modern world either. In conversations with his brother, he never failed to remind him that the majority of the great iconic inventions of our time were French: photography, cinematography, cars, aviation, chip and pin cards and even the domestic internet, with its predecessor the Minitel. According to Pierre, this country, which had led the rest of the world, had routinely done its best to let everyone else steal its ideas and patents, so that it hardly benefited from them and roundly forgot them – adding to the general negligence that lay at the root of the country's problems.

In the last weeks of his life, the shop increasingly represented to him one of the last surviving fragments of the past, a kind of island separated from the modern world by no more than a big sheet of glass. Soon passers-by would stop and stare, not to look at any of the items on display before coming in to enquire about the price, but to watch Pierre against the backdrop of the shop, like the waxwork models improperly named 'tableaux vivants' at the Musée Grevin. Pierre's waxwork figure would be captioned 'A man from the olden days'. You could observe him sitting at his Mazarin bureau, reading an old Léo Larguier book by the light of an Empire-style Bouillotte lamp, surrounded by furniture and unusual objects whose purpose nobody knew any more. He had spent so long selling curiosities, he had become one himself.

It seemed to JBM as if the futures of the two brothers had somehow been fixed that early afternoon as they stood at the crossroads leading back to school. They had separated on the pavement and, if the sequence could be played back now, you would see JBM walking towards a trench that had been dug in the road, and Pierre heading for the window of an antique shop. Having spent the past several weeks with his nose buried inside a biography of Napoleon, Pierre had been captivated by the sight of a snuffbox that, according to the sign in the window, had been carved out of the wood of a tree cut down on St Helena at the site of the Emperor's tomb. While Pierre stood transfixed by this relic which had passed through many hands over a century and a half, JBM could not take his eyes off the trench, freshly dug by pneumatic drill. Thick black cables lay alongside thinner red ones, tumbling together in neatly entwined braids before disappearing into the earth. JBM looked up at the surrounding buildings. These cables must feed the blocks of flats with electricity, powering the televisions, radios and telephones of every flat. This scalpel cut in the skin of the city was proof that when it came down to it, Paris was simply an enormous body, an organ with nerves, veins and muscles he could almost feel pumping beneath his feet. His vision extended to the whole neighbourhood, the *arrondissement*, then the metropolitan area, the country and the world, which he thought of in terms of a tennis ball, slightly flattened at the two poles, floating weightlessly, its electronic circuits functioning like neurons at the four cardinal points in a constant flow of information, images, voices and light.

Whoever entered this flux would control the future. Everything would happen via screens that would receive data within the home, not like televisions with their set schedules, but a different kind of screen, screens on which you could transmit images from one side of the globe to the other, images you had made yourself and wanted to share with people you knew or with complete strangers. And not only images, but words. Letters, novels, encyclopedias, newspaper articles, messages. People would be able to talk on screen. Anything was possible, because all the wires already existed – it was simply a matter of changing their contents and speed. That Christmas of 1973, Pierre asked for a cheque which, combined with his savings, would allow him to purchase the Emperor's snuffbox. JBM asked for the same thing, to buy his first books on computing. Each boy took to his bedroom to study his own destiny, Pierre holding a magnifying glass to every little detail of his precious acquisition, JBM annotating books with such esoteric titles as *Thyristors and TRIACs: Electronic Circuits no. 4* and *Digital Integrated Circuits* by Henri Lilen. He knew he would never be a great programmer, but he at least wanted to understand the theory before moving on to the next stage.

JBM's admiration for his brother never waned. He always considered Pierre to be the talented one. So talented, he had even written song lyrics. Yes, they were in English and the chorus was borrowed from Shakespeare, but he had done it. All JBM had done was to finance the recording. All that was left of Pierre now was a porphyry urn sitting behind the strong door of a safety deposit box belonging to JBM. Pierre had requested in his will that his ashes be scattered 'in a place of beauty and history' of his brother's choosing. JBM had still not found the place.

Au Temps Passé

'Excuse me, Monsieur, there's a notice that says "Closed for good" on your neighbour's shop.'

The owner of the shop next door was smoking a cigarette in his doorway, but he didn't reply.

So Alain pressed on. 'I can see that behind the curtain everything is still in the shop. Has he moved recently?'

'Yes,' replied the man slowly, drawing on his cigarette, 'he has moved, but not recently.'

'Do you know where I can reach him?'

'In an urn, if he's still there.'

'Excuse me?'

The man took a deep breath then explained. 'He's dead, Monsieur, a year ago. Did you know him?'

'Yes, but I hadn't seen him for a long time. Did he have an accident?'

'An artistic accident, yes,' murmured the neighbour, before telling the full story.

Pierre was known for his staged window displays, and the final one had been a corker. In the middle of the night, the antiquarian had lain down in the magnificent eighteenth-century bathtub that had been on display in the window for some weeks. Then he had overdosed on barbiturates. The next morning, passers-by had been treated to an arresting sight: the bath partly covered by a white sheet, Pierre's head in an old-fashioned bathing turban resting on his shoulder, and his right hand trailing on the floor holding a pen. His left arm rested on a plank covered in green material and held a farewell letter which his brother was later to read out at the funeral. Pierre had reproduced David's famous painting *The Death of Marat* down to the last detail.

'I will say it created quite a stir,' concluded the shop owner.

According to him, JBM had pulled strings to ensure that no hint of the macabre staging had appeared in the press, and particularly not in *Le Parisien*, which was known to have a voracious appetite for that sort of story. Freelance journalists who had started to prepare articles must have been told by their editors that it would not be worth their while to pursue them since they would be neither published nor paid for – orders from 'above'.

'I saw his brother twice,' went on the neighbour. 'He came, opened the grille, then closed it again, stayed for an hour and left again. He still pays the rent and the telephone bill; I sometimes hear the phone ringing through the wall. Along with some of the other shops, I've sent him an email asking if he plans to sell up, but he hasn't replied. It's not that we want to buy it given current conditions, it's because a phone shop was interested and that would attract customers.' The neighbour sighed before flicking his cigarette butt neatly into the gutter and going back indoors.

Alain heard his door close and made for the nearest café where he immediately ordered a rum.

So, Pierre the antique dealer, the man who had been passionate about the past and whom Alain had admired for his cultural knowledge and anecdotes about France, had put an end to it all. No doubt an accumulation of problems both private and professional had led him to do it, yet Alain felt that Pierre's death represented more than just a personal tragedy. The way he had deliberately stepped out of his own era by staging his death in that ostentatious way was a mark of something more profound. 'An artistic accident,' the shopkeeper next door had said. Pierre's trade was too slow – a trade where you spent entire afternoons daydreaming, or buried deep in art books whilst waiting for an erudite customer or the phone to ring, was out of step with modern life. The rhythm of the world had accelerated; everything had to happen quickly. The past and the aspect of culture Pierre had chosen to make a career out of, had less and less relevance to how people lived now. Frankly, thought Alain, sipping his rum, who now knew anything about Louis XIII and what he had done? Everybody knew Louis XIV because of the chateau and gardens of Versailles, Louis XVI because he'd ended up on the scaffold and Napoleon because of his hat, his wars and his exile on St Helena. All the rest of history, whether political or artistic, was just a shapeless mass which had over the course of time created the France of today and of which its citizens had only a hazy knowledge … Alain paid for the rum then checked his emails on his phone.

Quite unexpectedly, Frédéric Lejeune had already replied. Even though Thailand was on the other side of the world, there was only a five-hour time difference with France. Never having got on particularly well with Frédéric – they hadn't had a lot in common back in the days of the band – Alain had decided to come straight to the point about the cassette and had not mentioned the letter from Polydor. In response to his email, Frédéric did not say anything about the cassette but announced that he would soon be in France.

Hi Alain,

Great to hear from you. Good timing as well because I'm coming to Paris in a few days for a week so that I can finalise the sale of my parents' apartment in La Garenne-Colombes. I see from the internet that you're still a doctor and wondered if I could show you a boil on my left buttock? I've had it for two weeks and it's still very inflamed. I can't find a cream here that's any use and after a fourteen-hour flight, it's bound to be worse. Thank you in advance for your help with this. I have attached a photo of the boil — it's about as big as a ten-baht piece, so I suppose the size of a euro or maybe a two-euro piece.

See you soon, Fred.

Alain clicked on the photo of the boil, which filled his iPhone screen in all its glory, making him quickly close it. Digital technology had really transformed modes of communication. You asked someone a question and in reply received a huge photo of their buttocks. The fleeting dermatological image that had appeared on his screen confirmed what he had been thinking — Pierre Mazart, even though he had chosen a rather radical way of showing it, really did have no connection at all with the present day.

Bubble

At eleven o'clock in the evening, powered by the generator, the enormous tubes were filling with helium to the sound of the purring blower. Standing in his trademark overalls, Stan Lepelle surveyed the installation of his work. Situated at the entrance to the Tuileries Gardens on the octagonal basin sixty metres across, *Bubble* was taking shape before the very eyes of its creator.

'Everything going well?' the attaché from the Ministry of Culture asked obsequiously.

'Yes, very well,' replied Lepelle. 'Be careful fixing the base!' he called to the workmen who were putting steel protectors round thick ropes. These were attached to stakes that had been driven into the ground by an astonishingly noisy machine once the gardens had closed for the evening.

Lepelle walked round the structure. The pink, semi-transparent skin was very slowly inflating. It was made from the very latest synthetic rubber, BN657, which had been chosen because it was very thin but very strong. It would take a good hour to fill the thousand cubic metres. He went back to sit on the little folding chair that someone had set up for him under a light with its own projector linked to the generator.

'Would you like coffee?' he was asked by a young intern from the Ministry of Culture.

'I would, yes,' replied Lepelle.

He unfolded a copy of the article from his press office that was to appear in *Le Monde* the next day, and prepared to read the interview he had given recently. It filled a whole page. A 3D image of *Bubble* in the Tuileries as it would look by day and by night appeared next to his photo, in which he wore the frowning preoccupied expression of the intellectual engaged with the big questions of the day. The young girl brought his coffee. 'Sugar?'

'No sugar, ever,' he replied.

He grabbed the cup and continued reading.

The headline across the top of the page read 'The consecration of Stan Lepelle'. 'The work is intended to pose questions' was one of the quotes in bold in the body of the article. Lepelle stated crisply that 'the role of art is to question behaviour and the moral and ideological foundations of society'. The 25-metre-high, 60-metre-wide inflatable structure, a reproduction of his brain from a model generated by a 3D printer based on a medical scan, was not merely an artefact. It was a 'semantic question mark'. Further on in the article, he had managed to get in the fact that *Bubble* must provide a 'dialogue' with the Obelisk. That was important; you always had to have the word 'dialogue' in an interview about a contemporary art installation. It made the work seem appealing. Who would want to attack someone who just wanted to start a dialogue? No one.

The interview with *Le Monde* was the only one he would give and tomorrow all the press would be talking about it. By his silence he would communicate his scorn for future detractors, whilst also building his reputation as inaccessible. 'You have to make yourself appear unobtainable,' his dealer was always telling him. Not that Lepelle needed that cretin to point it out. Love it or hate it, no one would be indifferent to *Bubble*. There would be a hue and cry from some right-wing extremists – the ones who had unhooked McCarthy's butt plug from its air source or vandalised Anish Kapoor's *Dirty Corner* at Château de Versailles. But *Bubble* had no sexual connotation and that would make it harder for them. The extremists would make just enough fuss to publicise *Bubble*, his dealer said, but would stop short of vandalising it. In any case, the *mairie* had allocated two security guards who would do the rounds of the park at night so that during the month the installation was there, no joker could come and damage it.

Lepelle looked up from the newspaper at the work which was taking shape: a giant brain, his own brain, 60 metres across and 25 metres high, installed over the pond, filled with helium but solidly anchored to the ground. The gas was part of the symbolism of *Bubble*: 'the possibility of flight countered by support cables, or, if you prefer, desire and reason in apposition' had been his explanation to the journalist. When the brain was fully inflated, the din of the blower would cease and all that would remain to be done was the testing of the final phase of the installation. On the dot of midnight, the machinery designed by Matra Horlogerie and LED lighting would make the brain glow pink and blue. Lepelle got up from the chair and took a few steps back to savour this night alone with his statement piece.

A little shadow moved in the distance, then another. The two shadows froze, without taking flight. Cats would already have scarpered into the bushes. But these two silhouettes, nose to nose, seemed almost to be plotting in the glare of the spotlights. One of them was picked out by the light, revealing its red eyes. Lepelle recoiled in shock – rats. 'Shit,' he murmured. The rats hadn't moved a centimetre, and he could make out a third one coming from further away to join them. For more than a year, the gardens had been infested by rodents around the Place du Carrousel. They could quite often be seen amongst the walkers, pouncing on a bit of sandwich dropped by tourists before scurrying off, or busily crossing a lawn oblivious to the passers-by who stopped, horrified, in their path. The park authorities had tried to get rid of them, without success. Now the rats had come to reconnoitre what was happening so noisily in the middle of the night on their patch. Lepelle picked up a stone and threw it at them. One of the rats fled, whilst the albino with red eyes emitted a sort of sharp squeak, wrinkling its nose, and calmly set off towards a dark corner. Lepelle had the disagreeable impression that the rodent had given him a sardonic smile intended to convey, 'We'll be seeing each other again.'

Lepelle turned back to the pond. The first arabesques characteristic of brain matter were beginning to appear one after the other on the immense rubberised brain.

Agitprop

Domitile Kavanski's questionnaire had arrived by email. A list of seventeen questions going from the personal to the general that Aurore had downloaded to her tablet. JBM had initially refused to take part, stating plainly, 'That crazy woman's a pain in the arse.' Aurore managed to persuade him to spend a quarter of an hour answering it with her, like a child being forced to do his holiday homework on an August afternoon before he's allowed to go to the beach. Except that there would be no beach.

Things had not got off to a particularly good start with the high priestess of comms. On Blanche's orders, JBM had reluctantly attended his first 'informal chat', at which he had been shown a short film. A series of vox pops had been carefully put together before being presented to their subject. In the first clip, a man of North African origin selling fruit and veg on a market stall claimed that what the country was crying out for was JBM. 'We're counting on you, JBM!' he concluded, pumping his fists and smiling into the camera as if addressing a football player before the match. An old man leaning on the counter of a bistro with a small white wine in front of him also said JBM might be just what the country needed, because everyone was tired of the usual politicians, who never got anything done, and if we carried on with the same old same old, the elections would be 'a walk in the park for the far right'. He seemed quite proud of his little summary, and two other men at the bar nodded approvingly. Then they all held their glasses – two small white wines and a half of beer – and raised them to the camera: 'To JBM!' A woman in her forties fumed in front of the lens. 'We're always paying all these taxes and then they tell us there's no money. Where's it all going then? There's never been so many homeless. There, look at him.' The camera spun round to focus on a haggard-looking man sitting cross-legged on the pavement in front of a tent. 'For over a year, when I look out of my windows, I've seen him there. Can't they find him a job? They could give him a rake and a shovel and some work in a park. Don't tell me you need forty different degrees to look after a lawn and plant a few things! So, yes, yes, if he's going to get a grip on it all, I'll vote for him.' Finally, a girl with several piercings and a mouthful of chewing gum said she was yet to vote in an election, but if she did, it would definitely be for him because he seemed 'cool' and 'not like the others'.

The picture gently faded to black and, as if by magic, the giant screen rolled back up to the ceiling in the publicist's spacious office. JBM and Aurore turned to look at Domitile, who was sitting at the enormous oval table surrounded by her troops, silently congratulating herself.

'Who's been telling them I'm planning to stand for anything?' JBM asked coolly.

'Their hearts are telling them!' Domitile replied with such pizzazz it made you want to slap her. 'Their hearts, JBM,' she went on. 'You're the one they want. They're crying out for you.'

'Well, you can tell them I'm not a cardiologist. I'm not about to launch a political career just because a couple of housewives, three old sots and a Moroccan greengrocer have got it into their heads that they could see me in the Élysée.'

Domitile smiled and walked over to him, her stilettos clacking on the floor.

'I love it when you get angry, JBM,' she said, placing her hand on his shoulder before simpering, 'You must have been impossible as a child.'

She slowly moved away before suddenly swivelling back to face him.

'France is at your feet – don't you want it? Don't you want it, JBM?' she pressed him, raising her voice.

JBM left the screening, waving goodbye to everyone round the table. He shook hands with Domitile, who gazed seductively up at him, whispering mischievously, '*Au revoir, Président.*' He had barely left the building when she turned back to face her team and slammed her hand down on the table, making all eighteen people gathered around it jump out of their seats.

'Agitprop!' she shrieked. 'I want stories planted everywhere in the press. Get me all the actresses; ask them to tell us about whatever crappy film they've been in lately, their beauty tips, holiday plans, the kids, and throw in a political question to which the answer can only be 'JBM'. In return we'll get them ads, clothes, perfume, holidays, flat-screen TVs, partnership deals. We have to be everywhere, except the political arena – we'll attack from the inside. They're waiting for us on the beaches; we'll surprise them on the battlefields! I want to make people think. I want this to get inside their heads. He's the next occupant of the Élysée palace, him and him alone. Everybody got that?'

She raised to her lips an e-cigarette covered in a silver sheath which had been specially made for her by Cartier and engraved with her motto: 'Where next?' She strolled over to the window and gazed out at the city, which looked like a toy town from up here on the eighteenth floor.

'He doesn't seem too sure about it,' ventured one of the young men in the room.

'Let me worry about him,' Domitile said nonchalantly, as swirls of electronic smoke curled out from her crimson lips.

The questionnaire covered all kinds of subjects, from JBM's favourite writers and animals to his position on big questions such as the right to die or gay adoptions. Having already answered nine questions, JBM began dictating his response to the tenth.

'Pepe Mujica and his three-legged dog.'

'Hang on, JBM. You can't say Pepe Mujica. She'll have a fit.'

'Why not?'

'Just say Mitterrand or de Gaulle.'

'No, Aurore, no way. I'm going to give an honest answer to her question: which politician has made the biggest impression on you?'

Aurore put down her tablet with a sigh and went towards the window.

'Do you want me to put Mitterrand?' asked JBM conciliatorily.

'No, put Mujica and his dog. You're right; it's more original.'

It was true that the former Uruguayan president would be a more unexpected response than the names of either of the two great presidents of the French Fifth Republic. Jailed for thirteen years by the military dictatorship, during which time he had been tortured and thrown down a well, the former leader of the Tupamoros guerrilla group had gone on to rebuild his life, culminating in his election as his country's president at the age of seventy-four. Describing himself as 'a humble peasant', the little round man with the moustache, defined by the press – who can never resist a good catchphrase – as 'the poorest president on the planet', stood out among world statesmen for his refusal to embrace the high life. Rather than move into the presidential palace, he had carried on living on his little farm on the outskirts of Montevideo and donated most of his salary to charitable organisations or small businesses, keeping for himself a salary equivalent to the Uruguayan national average. Upon leaving office in 2015, he set up a small business selling home-grown flowers. During Mujica's five-year term, JBM had closely followed the speeches the president made at the UN and the interviews he had given from his modest home. Mujica called for people to open their eyes to the spread of consumerism, the rising tide of globalisation and the market economy that curtailed freedoms, making people slaves to their credit cards, working only to pay off the debts they had racked up buying things they didn't need. As he saw it, a poor man was not someone with few possessions, but someone who needed endless quantities of stuff and was never satisfied. Sitting at his farmhouse table, surrounded by books, he quoted philosophers like Epicurus and Seneca. He was also seen walking along mud paths with his little limping dog, who was missing a leg.

'You don't know what these people are like, Aurore. Domitile Kavanski is like a tick on a dog's back. If you want to get rid of it, you have to cut it out.'

'Can I ask you a question?'

JBM looked up.

'What if she's right? What if Blanche is right? And Bourdin? What if it's you, JBM, and we've come full circle. What if politicians as we know them are no longer equipped to face

82

the world we live in, they're outdated, over, and it's people like you who need to take control? I mean it,' she said, moving towards the desk. 'The candidates going for the presidency in six months' time don't have a quarter of your experience, or a diary or contacts book a tenth as full as yours. You, Bernard Arnault, François Pinault and Xavier Niel have more power and expertise between you than the whole political class of this country.'

'You'd like the government to be made up of businessmen?' JBM asked, smiling awkwardly. 'I can't see the French getting behind that idea.'

'You're trying to dodge the question, but seriously, I mean, who is François Larnier? He went to the École Nationale d'Administration, and then what? He's a member of parliament and leader of his party; he's only been a minister once, fifteen years ago; but really, take him out of the political machine, take him away from his constituents, and who is he? What does he know about the world we live in?' Aurore raged. 'He has thirty-five years in politics behind him; he should be thinking about retiring, but no, he's going after the biggest job of his career. It's unbelievable when you think about it! And he doesn't even speak English.'

In the Land of Smiles

'You must boost your intestinal flora,' Alain had just told his patient who was nodding seriously, when Maryam knocked.

'Come in!'

Maryam popped her head round the door. 'Monsieur Lejeune is here.'

'Perfect. Ask him to wait; I'll see him in five minutes.'

That's what Alain had suggested. That Frédéric should come to his consulting room when he arrived in France, make himself known to the receptionist and Alain would see him between two patients without him having to wait his turn in the waiting room.

When he accompanied his gut patient to the door, Alain did not recognise the man sitting in the hall who rose as he appeared. Bald on top, with quite long grey-white hair on either side, like Léo Ferré, he wore little glasses with red plastic frames and a large puffa jacket. He looked like an old left-wing maths teacher. They shook hands. 'Hi there,' said Frédéric. As Alain greeted Lejeune, he studied his face, trying to find the features of the blond young man who had played the melody of 'Such Stuff as Dreams Are Made On' on the synthesiser. In vain. If he'd been waiting for the bus beside this fellow, he would never have recognised his old friend. I hope I haven't aged as much as that, he thought, showing him into the surgery.

'Good flight?' Alain asked, just to say something.

'Yes, I arrived yesterday. It's been six years since I was last here. They're always long, these flights, but I take sleeping pills and just sleep, so they go quickly.'

Alain nodded. 'You're here for the week, is that it?'

'Yes, to sell my parents' apartment. I lost my parents ten years ago.'

Alain considered it was a bit too late to offer condolences so instead he frowned sympathetically.

'After they died, my sister and I had a tenant,' Frédéric explained. 'He was really reliable and stayed for five years, but when he left we had tenant after tenant and sometimes there was no one for months. My sister lives in Strasbourg, and I'm in Koh Samui, you see, so it was getting a bit complicated to manage.' He paused for a moment, scratching his neck. 'We decided to sell it last year. It's taken us a year to find a buyer. Can you believe it? A year! And we didn't get the price we wanted, even though it's a great flat in a modern building with bay windows. The estate agent says it's not easy to sell that kind of property, that people don't want to live in those areas now. It's true, La Garenne-Colombes does make you want to kill yourself. Thank goodness I don't live in France any more! I tell you, everyone here looks miserable; everyone is unpleasant. I'm staying with my sister in a little hotel near Gare du Nord until the papers are signed for the sale. The receptionist is about as cheery as an undertaker and no one even offered to carry our bags. We went out for dinner in a brasserie, and it was €38 each just for an egg mayonnaise and a vile steak with soft fries. Honestly, that's 230 francs, which is 1500 baht. For that amount at my hotel, you can have a marriage banquet! A whole fish, with drinks included, is

300 baht, €7.50, and it will be brought to your straw hut on the beach with a smile and a flower on the fish! Seriously, I tell you, you have to be mad to live here.'

Alain nodded. He had no opinion on the matter, had never been to Thailand, nor anywhere else in Asia.

'In Thailand, everyone smiles at you,' Frédéric continued. 'It's known as the Land of Smiles, and there's a reason for that. All the Thai people are so kind, but it's difficult to imagine that here. Here everything is dirty and ugly, the streets are disgusting. Aren't there any street cleaners in France or what? Or maybe people have become pigs … In Thailand you don't drop things in the street like that; people have respect, respect for nature and for each other.'

Alain listened calmly to this anti-France diatribe. Lejeune was expressing the view often held by those who have chosen to go and live somewhere hot (Morocco, Tunisia …) or else in the land of Asian Zen (Thailand, Bali …) He had a retired patient who had gone to live in Senegal with other French people who had grouped together in a sort of residential ghetto. He also raved about the good temper of the Senegalese and the blue skies.

'Were you able to find the cassette?' asked Alain, putting an end to the subject.

'No,' replied Frédéric. 'I even went to the trouble of looking in my parents' cellar for you yesterday, just in case, but I don't have it any more – I must have thrown it away.'

Alain nodded.

'Do you still muck about on electric guitar?' said Frédéric, suddenly animated.

'No. I still have the Gibson at the back of a cupboard, but I don't play it any more. And you?'

'From time to time I get out the synthesiser in the evenings,' replied Frédéric enthusiastically. 'After dinner, I have guests who like to dance under the stars.'

Alain pictured him dressed in a sarong, his bare feet in sandals, standing in front of a Bontempi organ playing old favourites like 'My Way' or 'Petite Fleur' as his French guests undulated under the Chinese lanterns. A pathetic image.

'My son disappeared three months ago,' Frédéric said suddenly. 'He converted to Islam last year. Sometimes I wonder if he went to Syria, and one day I'll see the little bugger's photo on CNN with a beard and a Kalashnikov … I'm going to remarry, a Thai girl; I've been separated from my wife for two years. She went off with a guy from the embasssy.'

Alain nodded again. He had no idea what to say to this person whom in fact he didn't know at all and who did not have the Holograms cassette. 'So why don't you show me your boil?'

Frédéric needed no second bidding to take his trousers down and show Alain the boil. The protuberance had indeed worsened.

'Why do you want to listen to our songs again?' Frédéric asked, his trousers round his ankles.

'No particular reason. It's for my children – they asked me – and because I remember our songs fondly. I'm going to give you some antibiotics and two different creams.'

'You know, they can't have been that good, our tracks, otherwise we would have had a response and a meeting with one of the record labels. Don't you think?'

'You're probably right.'

'And the others?' asked Frédéric, sitting back down. 'Do you have any news of them?'

Alain looked at him. What good would it do to explain that France was wondering if JBM would be their next president and that his brother had staged *The Death of Marat* in his own shop window? 'No news,' he said, beginning to write out the prescription.

Maybe it was Frédéric who had the right idea: rather than exhausting oneself for nothing over here, why not go and live in a beautiful country surrounded by lovely people?

'What do I owe you?' asked Frédéric, as he rose to leave.

'Are you joking? Nothing, of course,' replied Alain in a comradely tone. Then he accompanied him to the door. 'Good luck, Frédéric, and look after that boil.'

'Let me know if you're ever in Koh Samui.'

Alain was about to say that he would when Frédéric touched his arm and said with a knowing air, 'We're really looking our age now, aren't we? Good to see you.'

Alain was left speechless. Slowly Maryam looked up at him, but he had already gone back into his surgery and briskly closed the door.

'The Black Billiard,' said the voice.

'Hello,' replied Alain, 'I'd like to speak to Sébastien Vaugan.'

Silence on the other end. 'And you are?' the voice eventually asked condescendingly.

Alain could well imagine the well-heeled young person, most likely from the Groupe Union Défense, who was patronising him as some unknown wanting to be put through to the boss, just like that, on the telephone.

'If he's there, tell him that Alain Massoulier would like to talk to him.'

'Alain Massoulier,' repeated the voice. 'And you are what, a political journalist? Why are you calling?'

Alain controlled himself but could not prevent himself from

shooting back, 'I am Alain Massoulier, an old mate of Sébastien Vaugan; we used to call him "Fat Séb" before he took up weights. Will that do?'

There was silence again, until the voice said, 'I'll go and see if the Commander is free.'

Alain heard the receiver being laid down. 'Commander ...' he murmured.

'Hey, Massoulier!' cried Vaugan into the phone. 'You coming for your glass of wine? Haven't seen you for ages – what is it, four years? Five years?'

'It's six,' Alain corrected him. He wasn't likely to forget their last encounter in a hurry. Alain had been dining in a restaurant at a table with twenty other GPs. They were already on their main course, and the conversation was turning to the latest generic drugs, when Vaugan made his entrance to the brasserie, surrounded by ten of his men, shaven-headed in black polo necks and leather coats. 'Look, it's Vaugan,' murmured one of the doctors, leaning towards his colleagues. Vaugan's gaze swept the brasserie in imperious fashion before resting on Alain, who paled as he saw him approach, hand outstretched. 'What a surprise. Are you well, my friend?' The handshake had been firm and virile. 'I'm fine and you ...?' Alain had muttered. 'Really good, as usual. You'll have to stop by one of these days and we'll have a glass of wine together.' 'Yes, I'll give you a ring,' Alain murmured. Vaugan had taken his leave with an 'Enjoy your meal, Messieurs,' that sounded like a command, and gone to join his bodyguards at the far end of the restaurant. When Alain looked round, his colleagues were staring at him. 'We ... we were at school together, a long time ago,' lied Alain in a tone he hoped was casual, and that seemed to satisfy the assembled company. 'I seem destined to keep running into him about once every six years, totally by chance – don't ask me why, that's just the way it is.' The matter was closed and the talk turned again to drugs.

This time, it had again been six years, but it was Alain who was asking for the meeting.

'What can I do for you?'

'I just wanted to ask you something.'

'Something? That's a bit vague.'

'I could come and see you at your …' Alain wasn't sure what the correct word was … 'Bar? Billiard academy? Headquarters?'

'At my campaign HQ,' supplied Vaugan proudly.

'You're running a campaign?'

'Very soon. Everything is changing. Come whenever you like; I'll tell my staff to let you in.'

And he hung up.

Roosevelt vs. Louis XV

'An airport runway?' suggested a young man with longish hair.

'Too elitist, too cryptic,' replied Domitile Kavanski.

'Fields, vineyards, the countryside ...' threw in another man with a hipster look: huge beard, undercut, and tortoiseshell glasses.

Domitile tutted irritably.

'And a Romanesque church in the background perhaps?' she asked. 'You're not getting it. That screams "Mitterrand".'

'How about the sea then?' put in someone else.

'No, the sea's too scary, too big, too powerful.'

Domitile sat back in her leather armchair to take a good look at her team, puffing all the while on her electronic cigarette.

'The sky?' hazarded another young man.

'No!' Domitile fumed. 'We need some kind of man-made construction, something that embodies the future, something symbolic, recognisable to the masses. Use your brains, for the love of God!'

For the past hour, they had been putting forward ideas for the double-page photo spread that would open the piece on JBM in *Paris Match*. Domitile had landed six pages in the weekly magazine and was putting in place her CCP strategy (Connection/Confidence/Policies). On the last two points, JBM was always ranked very highly. There was work to do on the 'connection' side of things. In the opinion polls she had commissioned, JBM was described as enigmatic, reserved and aloof. He would have to lose that image. When it came to the 'fun' questions, many of those surveyed replied that if JBM was an animal, he would be a cat. It was tiresome, this cat thing. As far as Domitile was concerned, a cat was an overly complicated animal: it wouldn't come when you called it; you couldn't find it when you looked for it; it ran away when you tried to stroke it. In short, cats were a pain in the arse.

'The Eiffel Tower?' suggested a young woman with a ponytail.

Domitile closed her eyes.

'Get out, Priscilla,' she said. 'Get out. I can't bear listening to such tripe.'

The woman stood up and left the room, quietly closing the door behind her.

'Now, let's think,' Domitile said coldly. 'Let's get our neurons working. There are seven of us left in this room. There are a hundred billion neurons in every person. I'll let you work out the brain power we're drawing on.'

'A motorway ...?'

'No, pollution, noise – doesn't work. The road idea is good – it carries the values we want to convey – but motorways are horrible.'

'A bridge?'

Domitile took a drag of electronic smoke. The young man almost thought he had it, when she shook her head.

'Too loaded. People will recognise the bridge. It'll be linked to some provincial backwater. What the hell would JBM want with the Pont du Gard or the Millau viaduct? It makes no sense. Seems like a good idea, but it isn't.'

'A station platform? Or railway lines?' suggested a young woman. 'Railway lines coming out of a big station, without showing which one it is.'

Domitile slowly looked up and stared at the woman for a moment.

'Yes,' she murmured. 'Yes, that's it. A railway line towards the future. That's the killer image! Trains are the transport of the masses, but they also have a whiff of luxury. They're a symbol of industry serving the people. You, you and you,' she said, pointing at various people, 'and you, of course,' she added, addressing the girl whose idea it was, 'take your phones and go to every train station in Paris. Get me pictures of railway lines and platforms. I want you back here within three hours. Jump to it!'

The four chosen ones grabbed their bags and left the room.

'Railway lines ...' she murmured, ecstatic, rocking back and forth in her chair, 'blurred out in the background of the image, amazing ... A man on the go, in the driving seat. It's pure harmony: he's the man driving France's train, he's the locomotive; he's the driver, the machine, and the man serving others.'

The remaining members of her audience were furiously taking notes.

'It's magnificent!' she cried, leaping to her feet.

A young man tried to interject.

'He does give Pepe Mujica as his answer to the question on—'

'Who cares what he said?' Domitile cut him off. 'It's not his answers we're interested in, it's ours. He's Roosevelt. Roosevelt vs. Louis XV. Our Roosevelt travels by train, Louis

XV by horse-drawn carriage. Can't you see we're writing a new history here?' She laid her hand gently on the desk. 'With new ink, a new sheet of paper and a new pen.'

All those nodding their heads knew exactly where Domitile was going with her curious allusion to the American president and his New Deal, in contrast to the last king of pre-revolutionary France: to the most highly spun presidential election of all time, that of François Mitterrand in 1981. For the first time, admen had led the campaign. There were three of them: Gérard Colé, Jacques Pilhan and Jacques Séguéla. The last of these became the French publicist most often seen in the media, but behind the scenes Colé and Pilhan were finessing the key points the election would turn on, as summarised in a secret note code-named 'Operation Roosevelt vs. Louis XV'. Their aim was to usher in a new social era and demonstrate that Valéry Giscard d'Estaing was a man of the past, a smooth talker who looked the part abroad, but no longer understood France, and was perhaps past caring, so sure was he of continuing to enjoy his favourite dish of warm foie gras at the table of the Élysée for a long time yet: he was Louis XV. At the other end of the scale, Mitterrand was supposed to symbolise renewal, dynamism, the future, and above all the image of a humble man with simple tastes, with principles, ideas and a vision – in the mould of the iconic president of the USA. The imagery created by Jacques Séguéla under the slogan 'La Force Tranquille', with the Socialist leader pictured calmly gazing ahead to the future with a little village church behind him, was the crowning element of the plan. François Mitterrand would go on to be president of France for fourteen years.

Domitile drew on her cigarette and announced her strategy in a single line.

'JBM, the man we didn't dare to expect, versus the men from whom we no longer expect anything.'

There was one small detail left to deal with. It was time to break down JBM's elusive image. Domitile had a plan: cookery.

A Beautiful Russian

Bubble had received good coverage in the press and on social media, but Lepelle had been disappointed by the public's reaction. Wrapped up in their own problems and worn down by the economic crisis, the fact was that Parisians had greeted the work with indifference. There had been a few modest demonstrations – never more than thirty people each time – at which there were placards reading 'This is where our taxes go!', 'IQ of Bubble = 0' and other such phrases painted on cardboard. These little groups came mainly from traditionalist Catholic associations – the children of those who used to rail against posters showing models revealing too much for their taste, or priests kissing nuns in adverts twenty-five years earlier. Killjoy nitpickers and quibblers.

Le Figaro had managed an opinion piece in which a respected old Academician had described *Bubble* as 'the obscene display to all and sundry of a megalomaniac's intimate organ'. But that was about all. In the short television reports about the installation, Lepelle had seen for himself how little interest it generated. 'It's fun,' many said. 'I can't see any problem with it,' several people had also commented, with an indifferent shrug. The comparison most often advanced had been aired on the one o'clock news by a journalist in his forties who said *Bubble* reminded him of Simon in *Captain Future*: 'You know, that flying blue brain that spoke, that was always in a little clear capsule above the Captain's shoulder.'

Lepelle was furious with these infantile forty-year-olds always referencing Japanese cartoons or *Star Wars*, the galactic epic that was their bible. What was worse, acting the reclusive artist had not paid off. He had made a mistake there and he was annoyed with himself. He should have done many more interviews and in particular he should have accepted Thierry Ardisson and Laurent Ruquier's offers. Instead he had sent a message to the two presenters via his gallery that the artist was 'devoting himself to his work' and would not be replying to any requests in the coming weeks. What an error! If you act mysterious and distant, people forget you. Even though the Minister for Culture was very satisfied with the installation, no one was going to be offering him such a prestigious site again any time soon.

One morning, Lepelle's dealer told him that he had heard Femen were going to stage a demonstration near the brain. *Bubble* represented a male brain, and the topless female activists were planning one of their anti-male-chauvinist displays at which they excelled. Lepelle had been delighted at the prospect of this unexpected publicity. But the days had passed and he had waited in vain. The hysterical blondes, their breasts garishly daubed with slogans, failed to materialise. 'What are the bitches waiting for?' he had emailed his dealer. 'I don't know – they must have changed their minds,' he replied.

Lepelle had also gone to the Tuileries Gardens incognito one afternoon to witness for himself the way people only looked at his work for a few seconds. Then they walked round it, pushing their buggies, or eating candyfloss in couples. They would have regarded a circus tent or hot-air balloon with more interest. Young Japanese girls took photos of themselves in front of it with fixed smiles, but they would have done the same with Pluto at Disneyland Paris. Most galling were the middle-management types returning to work through the gardens after their lunch break. They were in clusters of four or five, deep in conversation with each other, or more often on their mobiles. They didn't so much as glance at *Bubble*. Not for a moment. Had you asked them on the way out of the gardens if they had noticed anything unusual in the Tuileries, they would have said, 'No. Why?'

The most encouraging news came from Qatar. The organisers of the 2022 World Cup had made contact with Lepelle's art dealer to see if he would 'possibly consider designing an inflatable structure to be unveiled at the opening of the stadium'. On hearing of the Gulf's interest in his work, the artist immediately emailed his agent back, 'Take them for everything they've got!' He was already working up some ideas, notably a giant shoe stud of which he had made a model three metres high that now took centre stage in his studio. But he wasn't satisfied with it. Separated from its host, the stud was no longer identifiable. It could have been a depiction of a type of nail or peg, advertising a weekend tool promo at Castorama. Before the stud, he had thought of a giant inflatable ball-bladder filled with helium before realising that the original bladders used as balls were pig bladders and that to offer the Qataris a giant pork bladder for display at the entrance to their stadium might get him into all sorts of trouble.

'Are you just going to waste your life smoking joints from morning to night?' demanded Lepelle.

Ivana, stretched out on the sofa, turned to look at him, her pupils dilated.

One of these days he was going to have to ask her to pack her bags and leave. Quite soon, in fact. There were some advantages to living with a porn star, but there were also disadvantages. The main one being the cloud of smoke that constantly billowed through the ground floor of the house.

Lepelle had met her through his project *Sexus* – an explicit title for images that were indeed explicit. For some weeks he had considered the idea of moving away from large structures and producing instead large-scale digital photographs. A series of limited-edition images aimed at a rich clientele avid for modernity. The world revolved around money and sex, and Lepelle, not seeing how he could represent the first, had opted for the second. He had mined his contacts in search of two models, a boy and a girl, whom he could photograph as they made love. Someone had found him a young Russian girl who made porn films and who seemed to be inordinately expensive, and a pretentious young boy who was more modestly priced. Lepelle had organised sessions in his studio from which he had made a series of ten large boards, the images edited so that they were almost abstract, though it was still very clear what they depicted.

'What on earth are these?' his dealer had asked, looking through the series of photographs. 'Are you trying to wreck your reputation? Buren's known for his stripes, Annette Messager for hand-knitted animals in costumes, Warhol for colourised photo negatives, Lichtenstein for parody pop art, Damien Hirst for cows in formaldehyde. Your thing is giant structures. Stick to what you're good at and don't annoy me with this nonsense. You and all those others are identified with a style – do you want to kill the golden goose and me along with it? You're being completely irresponsible. Put this bullshit away; I never want to see it again.'

All that remained of this venture was Ivana who had come to stay with him for a week, and that had been six months ago. Ivana, with an accent you could cut with a knife and her terrible French. Ivana, who sometimes disappeared for several days before returning with no explanation. Lepelle suspected her of prostituting herself. Some of the luxury hotels of the capital had certainly seen her supple form passing furtively through their lobbies on the arm of one of her compatriots. Her porn films, of the more upmarket variety, provided her with an infallible calling card she could use whenever she liked. She could provide a real-life performance for a fee, with dinner, champagne and presents as well. Apart from the sex, the only benefit of having Ivana was that she did the shopping and her cooking was quite good. She also took care of the laundry. She was aesthetically very pleasing and his status was greatly enhanced by appearing with a six-foot consort at official cocktail parties. He enjoyed the look of panic on the faces of the other men when they understood that she was with him. That alone was worth putting up with her languor and her permanent state of intoxication. When she was not smoking a joint, she spent hours on Facebook or chatting in Russian on the phone, with her girlfriends or her lovers, he did not know. Lepelle couldn't tell because he spoke not a word of Russian. From time to time he heard her mention his name and wondered what she could be saying about him.

She came from a tiny godforsaken village in Siberia, so small it didn't appear on any map. When she showed him the photos on her phone of her friends back home who, like her, dreamt of becoming a model and had suffered mixed fortunes, he could not get over it. The strapping farmers with wrinkled faces and their babushkas with reddened cheeks had all produced these slender creatures with legs that went on for ever, translucent skin and practically perfect features. It was a genetic mutation. Ivana, the fisherman's daughter; Lena, the innkeeper's daughter; Yuliana, the daughter of the bus driver; Tania, the mayor's daughter; Anna, the woodcutter's daughter, any one of them could happily have graced the cover of *Vogue*. 'How many of you are there?' he had asked her anxiously as if someone had shown him a video diary of extraterrestrials.

One other little thing had struck him: one of her friends from the village, as beautiful as Ivana, had a scar on her right cheek. Ivana explained that her boyfriend had struck her with a stone when he heard that she also wanted to go for a model casting. He had done it one day when they went for a swim in the river. He had chosen an especially sharp stone and hit the young woman in the face. He had done it so that she wouldn't leave, so that no one would ever take her from him. According to Ivana, he had hidden himself away at his parents' and had cried for three days, and the girl had done the same at her parents' house. Then they had been reconciled and now everything was fine again.

The model agencies knew where to go for an abundance of beautiful girls. Once or twice a year, casting directors would visit these regions like latter-day trappers. Instead of rifles they were equipped with digital cameras and shot their game from every angle – not forgetting a shot of their teeth – then reported back to the agencies. From time to time, one of the girls really did become a model. The chosen girl would then do the rounds of photo shoots and society parties, gathering thousands of contacts. Then she would marry a rich man, bear him some children, and spend the rest of her life in a beautiful house in California with an infinity pool, staff and a home hairdresser. Other girls would try their luck as escorts or sales assistants. Some, like Ivana, did not achieve a breakthrough and moved seamlessly on to making porn films. They travelled and lived off men they utterly despised until they found one that pleased them. Or not. This was modern-day adventuring.

His computer pinged – an email from his art dealer: 'Hello Stan, Alain Massoulier rang. He said he knows you. And he also said something about a letter and a song – I didn't really understand. He's a doctor. He had already sent an email which I forgot to pass on to you, so here it is. See you soon.'

'Good news?' asked Ivana.

'An old friend would like to see me.'

'Well, you should invite him over then.'

'Hmm, maybe; he could turn out to be a pain in the neck – success always attracts people like that.'

Then he went and shut himself away in his studio. The giant stud stared at him, like a reproach, an insult to his creativity. Lepelle could feel it; he would be utterly incapable of coming up with anything at all for the Qataris.

The Commander

'Have you won the lottery?'

'Better than that, the EuroMillions,' replied Vaugan.

Alain was staring at him in disbelief when the noise of an electric saw filled the ground floor of the Black Billiard – what was left of it – making him jump. The tables had been consigned to the back, under dust sheets. The immense room with its moulded six-metre-high ceilings was undergoing a profound transformation. The French Billiards Academy founded in 1930 was closing its doors to re-open as the head office of 'France République'. A huge sign bearing these words along with the slogan 'To the Right of the Right' was leaning against a wall. Alain and Vaugan faced each other, comfortably installed in Chesterfield armchairs, the only pieces of furniture left from the old decor. They each had a glass of red wine in their hand, and several workmen were busy about the room. Vaugan's bodyguards, five young men with crew cuts and a young girl in military fatigues, had moved away when Alain arrived. They were now perched on bar stools, passing the time looking at their smartphones. The sawing stopped abruptly.

'Yes,' Vaugan was saying, swirling his wine, 'I'm not kidding, I really did win, no joke. The guy from the Paris region who trousered a hundred and forty million euros five months ago? That was me. I'm sponsored by the State now!' he cried. 'I'm a public utility! I've played that shitty game for thirty years, it's only fair that I'm the one. Just think it could have been an Islamist who won all that money.' He looked at Alain in a meaningful way. 'And what would he have used it all for? Have you thought of that?'

'I don't think they play the lotto,' Alain said tentatively.

'You never know,' objected Vaugan, 'but anyway, I was the winner. I've got more money than the Republicans and the Socialist Party put together. I bought this building, I'm putting my offices in at the top and I'm renaming the party. WWP won't do any more. I have a communications adviser working on it. It's that bastard who's also telling me I have to put on a suit and tie to appear on the telly. Because we've arrived. You know what I mean? We've arrived. And not just in France, all over Europe,' he said, his eyes shining. 'Everyone will follow us, even the Chinese, in fact especially the Chinese – they've grown up under the cosh; they understand about homeland and discipline. You know, it's only the Yanks and three or four European presidents who believe in democracy. Democracy, my arse! Look at what they've done in Iraq: a country which functioned, which existed, is now delivered into the hands of religious barbarians and gangs! We don't even know who runs Iraq. Same goes for Libya.'

Vaugan leant towards Alain and looked him straight in the eye. 'Kings, my friend, and dictators, that's all that works. Royalty or dictatorship. That's what liberates people.'

'But your party is called France République.'

'Yes, big joke!' laughed Vaugan. 'But no one is taken in,' he went on, before adding coldly, 'Tito, Saddam, Franco, Mussolini, Gaddafi – may they rest in peace – were all great men.'

'And Hitler?' asked Alain.

Vaugan fell back in his chair and looked at Alain with an amiable smile. 'You'll never change, will you?'

'So your plan is to become the dictator of France?' asked Alain in disbelief, before taking a sip of wine.

'Why not? I've got the profile, haven't I? I can go and talk to Putin, no problem; I can even talk to an American president, no problem. I speak very good English; I can explain France to him. I can tell him, "Our country is a thousand years old, yours has just been born. You're five centuries behind us, so you can shut up! You're in no position to give us lessons. Let's see where your America is in a thousand years, if it even exists."'

'That's a great way to introduce yourself to a head of state,' Alain commented soberly.

'Yes, I think it's excellent! It shows him what's what. Can you shut the fuck up with that noise? I can't hear myself speak!' Vaugan yelled at the workmen.

The building noises quietened down immediately.

'I can see that this is more than you can handle; you're living in the past. I don't blame you for that. We'll be putting in place re-education programmes for people like you.'

Alain looked at Vaugan, slouched in his armchair but absolutely certain of himself.

'You know we're a bit like 999 ...'

'999?'

'Yes,' replied Vaugan, drinking his wine. 'The number you dial for the police. Plenty of people hate the police, badmouth the police, but the day they find themselves in trouble, those same people are happy to dial 999 and see the police arrive. When the country is facing ruin, you'll be very glad to see me and my European comrades arriving with our flags, our straightforward ideas and our leather jackets. You will call on us, as always in the history of every great country. The radical right arrives and restores order at the request of the people.'

After a brief silence, Vaugan said, 'You wanted to ask me about "something".'

'It's nothing at all to do with your interests now, but I received this in the post.' Alain held out the envelope from Polydor.

Vaugan took out the letter, unfolded it and began to read.

'Bloody hell!' he murmured, then he smothered a sort of sharp chuckle. 'That's fucking terrible.'

He turned the envelope over and looked again at the postmark, holding it far from his eyes – thirty-three years late!

'It doesn't surprise me, there are so many blacks working for the Post Office. The last time I went there, it was like being in the Caribbean.'

Alain did not reply to that.

'Shit, mate. D'you realise what this means? It could have been us instead of Indochine; we could have played the Stade de France.'

The idea seemed to set him daydreaming. '*Sic transit gloria mundo*,' he said, handing the letter back to Alain, who corrected him. '*Gloria mundi*.'

'Same thing,' retorted Vaugan. 'Thus passes the glory of the world, ours too.'

'Do you think you might have the tape?'

'That was the "something" you wanted from me?' asked Vaugan, disappointed.

He made a sweeping gesture in the air with a look of disgust. 'It went up in smoke, the tape, and everything else with it. The Black Billiard almost burnt down three years ago. Allegedly an electrical problem in the cellars in the middle of the night. I don't really believe that. There are plenty of people who would like to make a bonfire out of this place. I had the most precious things in a safety deposit box at the bank, but I used to keep everything else here. And,' he said despondently, 'now I have nothing left, nothing at all. But I care about the past, my own and the past of France. The past, Alain: the struggles of the countryside and the churches, the little churches which are left abandoned with their leaking roofs and their young parish priests who get nothing for their trouble but a kick up the backside, whilst there are millions available to build new mosques. Have you ever thought about that, Alain? No, you don't give it a thought. Happily, there are people who do think about it, more and more of them. They think about it and it hurts them! Hang on; what I've just said is genius.'

He pulled a digital Dictaphone out of his pocket and repeated the phrase, then nodded in a satisfied way.

'I record everything; I always have this with me, this digital little gizmo. I record my interviews with journalists, and all my telephone conversations. As soon as I speak to someone, I start recording.'

'Are you recording us?' asked Alain nervously.

'Of course not,' said Vaugan, shrugging, 'it's not the same with you. You're not dangerous, you're nice – you're an old mate. And I'm going to do something for you. Kevin!'

One of the young men got down from his bar stool and came over.

'Get me two invitations to the Zénith for my good friend. We're launching the new party next week. There are hardly any places left,' said Vaugan proudly. 'Oh yes, we can fill the Zénith, no problem.' He gave a little click of the tongue. 'This is just the beginning.'

*

A few minutes later, after Alain had gone, the communications adviser came and sat in the chair he had vacated. He started to talk about the suit Vaugan should appear in: something very smart, dark grey with a light-grey tie, similar to what a banker might wear, but not exactly the same. A suit that said, 'Here is someone influential from a major city.' And lace-up shoes were essential, not loafers. Vaugan listened without really hearing. He was distracted by the letter that had been lost by the postal service and then reappeared. He couldn't help seeing himself in a vast dwelling in the LA Heights. With dozens of jukeboxes, bass guitars hanging on the walls, a magnificent swimming pool and deep sofas. It was a haven of peace when he was not on a world tour; he had gone much further than the Holograms and had played with numerous famous groups and artists. He was a renowned and respected bassist, as good as Pastorius and Tony Levin, maybe even Roger Waters. He had become a sort of myth. Sometimes, but rarely, he would give an interview to *Rock & Folk* or *Rolling Stone* from beside his swimming pool or in the bar of a grand hotel.

'So,' said the communications adviser, beaming, 'what do you say? It's going to be great, isn't it?'

Vaugan looked at him, wondering how much he paid this buffoon. There had been two things he had been determined on from the start: he wanted a big stage, high up, that he could speak from with a clip-on microphone, and even more importantly, he wanted his appearance to be heralded by the music from *Rocky III*, 'Eye of the Tiger'.

Meanwhile, Alain was seated on a café terrace with an espresso. He was watching the winter sun setting over the buildings as it bathed them in purple light. A man in a loden coat and elegant little tweed hat with a feather, like hunters wear, came and sat down at a neighbouring table and ordered coffee. He removed his suede gloves when the waiter brought him the cup and had a sip before he too was lost in contemplation of the sunset. Without taking his eyes from the buildings, he said, 'You seem like a nice man, Doctor.'

'I beg your pardon?' asked Alain. 'Do we know each other?'

'No,' replied the other, apparently regretfully, 'but can one ever really know another person? Restif de La Bretonne used to say, "When you look at someone, you only see half of what is there."'

There was silence between them and the man turned to Alain, fixing him with his pale-blue eyes, a smile on his lips.

'Who are you?' asked Alain. 'Special Branch? Homeland Security?'

The man's expression became nostalgic. 'Special Branch, counterintelligence, the secret services ... All that was over a long time ago. Vaugan gave you something – would you be so kind as to show it to me, Doctor?'

At first Alain wanted to refuse, feeling slightly indignant. There was, after all, no obligation for him to obey. But the entirely courteous way the man had formulated his request somehow made him want to acquiesce. He took the tickets from his coat pocket and held them out.

'Thank you,' said the man as he took them.

He looked at them for a moment. 'First row, prime position. Were you planning to attend?'

'Who knows?' replied Alain, defiantly.

The man nodded calmly then tore the tickets in two.

'Now, hang on,' said Alain. But that had no effect at all on the man in the little hat, who conscientiously finished his task, letting the scraps of paper fly off in the evening wind before saying, 'There are some excellent programmes on the television that evening.'

He took a ten-euro note from his wallet, tucked it under the saucer of his coffee cup. 'The coffee's on me.'

He got up, pulled on his suede gloves and bowed slightly. 'Delighted to have made your acquaintance.'

As he walked away, Alain wanted to shout after him, 'Hey! Where are you going? Come back!' But the words froze on his lips. The figure in the loden coat was met by a white car that came to a stop at his side. Alain thought it was an Audi, or maybe a Mercedes. The man got in and the car disappeared into the traffic.

Pot-au-feu

'Who are we kidding? I look like a total idiot,' JBM complained, pointing at the wooden spoon in his hand.

'You don't look like an idiot, JBM; you look like an ordinary Frenchman.'

As he stirred the bubbling *pot-au-feu* his cook had prepared for him, JBM looked up at Domitile. He had put on an apron, rolled up his shirtsleeves and taken off his cufflinks and Breguet chronometer watch.

'But I'm not an ordinary Frenchman. I'm one of the richest men in France,' replied JBM.

'Yes, but people don't know that and, if they find out, we'll just say it's not true, the figure's been exaggerated and, anyway, the fact that you're a man of means and yet still cook for yourself shows just what a good guy you are. Look at this kitchen,' said Domitile, spreading her arms wide, 'these lovely cupboards, spices, vegetables, this sunlight; everyone's going to want to come to your place and enjoy JBM's *pot-au-feu*! People will fantasise about you, women especially – you're the ideal man!' she squealed. 'The bon vivant who cooks the Sunday lunch while Madame lies on the sofa reading the *Femina* supplement and getting texts from her grown-up children ...'

'Give it a rest, will you, Domitile? All this nonsense is giving me a headache,' JBM hissed under his breath.

'Look happy,' ordered the photographer. 'Smile; that's it,

perfect. Let's do another one. Can you take a spoonful of stock and give it a taste?'

For half an hour, JBM had been stirring a now-overcooked *pot-au-feu* under the spotlights set up in the kitchen, to the constant flash of the camera. The domestic staff – the cook who had actually made the *pot-au-feu*, the butler and the housekeeper – had withdrawn discreetly to the doorway, where they stood watching Monsieur pretend to be an enthusiastic weekend cook, while doing their best not to smirk or nudge each other. Monsieur, who couldn't boil an egg and was barely capable of pouring himself a Nespresso from the machine.

'Who do you think I am, Alain Ducasse?' JBM said with irritation in his voice.

'He's right. Taste the stock – there you go, excellent. Look this way, well done ... that's perfect. Just like that! Fantastic! Smile, that's wonderful! That's exactly what we're looking for. We believe it, we're there with you, we're all going to eat your *pot-au-feu*!' squawked Domitile.

After the photo with the expertly diced vegetables, during which JBM had almost sliced through his thumb, and the one in the garden of the mansion in which he had had to place one hand on Blanche's shoulder and point up at the sky, with Blanche smiling up at whatever he was drawing her attention to – a pigeon, a plane, a fly, whatever; it was about them sharing the simple pleasures of the moment, while looking symbolically towards the future – and now they had reached the '*Pot-au-feu* sequence', the last before they were due to leave for Gare de Lyon to capture the shot of JBM in front of the railway lines that was sure to be a minor masterpiece. 'A six-page feature in *Match* is worth going to a bit of effort for,' as Domitile said.

Blanche had not taken part in the 'culinary moment', but had said goodbye to JBM and gone to Roissy. She was meeting some of her staff there to fly to New York for a few days to attend the annual board meeting of Caténac's American business.

JBM took advantage of a break in proceedings to join Aurore in the sitting room, where she was watching Vaugan on BFM-TV promoting the rally that was being held that night. He had swapped his usual black T-shirt for a suit and tie which looked tailor-made.

'I've got a message for the people of this country. I'm on a mission. I didn't set up France République to line my own pockets.'

'A party of the extreme right,' the journalist immediately bounced back.

Vaugan brushed the comment aside and went on to dismiss the entire political establishment and the elite *énarques* who ran the country. He proposed that their Alma Mater, the École Nationale d'Administration, be abolished and why not knock the building down too, since 'there aren't enough green spaces in our cities'.

Many people considered Vaugan to be a 'useful idiot', but JBM did not share that view. Instead, he saw him as one of those prophets of doom who spring up before a catastrophe.

The internet had allowed all kinds of fanatics to build themselves a reputation, or construct an entire persona. Through social networks and other free platforms, they could spread their ideas among a not inconsiderable number of followers, whose identities were hard to uncover. Back in the *other world* – the world before the digital revolution of the late twentieth century – these false prophets simply could not have existed. They would have had to rely on countless connections in order to get a pamphlet put out secretly and read by almost no one, or perhaps have had to self-publish and distribute their writings among a small circle confined to a couple of bistros and associations. They would never have found their way into the newspapers, still less onto TV screens. The creation of a parallel space stretching right round the globe had allowed Andy Warhol's prediction to come true: everyone really did have a chance at fifteen minutes of fame; singers, comedians and aspiring film stars had stepped into the breach, and ran their small businesses via paid websites and the various consumer products they offered for sale: CDs or DVDs, VOD, T-shirts, mugs, books, you name it. The lucky ones were picked up by producers and put to the test in front of an audience and cameras. Only a handful of them survived their emergence from the internet fishbowl and adapted to the oxygen of the real world, like fish emerging from Jurassic lakes with feet for walking on dry land. The best-case scenario was that one of them might go on to enjoy a career in pop for a few years. The worst would see a silly and narcissistic shampoo girl living the dream on reality TV shows and in celebrity magazines, before being spat out by the machine like a spent fuse.

And there was a darker element on the margins. Version 2.0 of the world had opened up to the new preachers. Whether religious or otherwise, they were all out to initiate a growing number of non-believers into the mysteries of modern life, to which they claimed to hold the key. Jihadists, fascists, conspiracy theorists, survivalists, anti-Zionists and other self-proclaimed experts mixed together a murky cocktail of political theories and alternative solutions. These new heretics were everywhere on the Net, and swept across the entire political and religious spectrum – aside from the Buddhists, who advocated a kind of good-natured shamanism that was close to Swiss-style neutrality.

Vaugan had successfully jostled for his position at the furthest end of the far right several years before, and had no intention of giving it up. He kept a weekly current affairs vlog on his group's website, in which he would appear alone in front of the camera, giving his point of view, his analyses and solutions with total impunity. He had come to the attention of the press and even TV execs, who had cautiously invited him to appear on a few late-night programmes. Vaugan had been smart enough to tone it down for the cameras, coming across as fairly level-headed and even quite smiley, like an ex-army uncle who initially seems scary but over the course of lunch turns out to be quite nice. When he was confronted with videos showing him ranting into the camera, he simply explained he was a hot-blooded man and that was a French quality. Vaugan had succeeded in bringing together disillusioned people of every stripe, from the most radical elements of the extreme right to Bible-bashers, by way of the dejected long-term unemployed, the angry, the paranoid, the bitter and the lost. Which, come to think of it, was quite a lot of people.

'Doing a good job, isn't he?'

JBM and Aurore turned towards Domitile, who had just entered the living room.

'He has a communications adviser,' she went on, 'David Bachau, one of my protégés. If I may say, that's why you need PR-ing too, JBM, and you don't have the pupil, but the master,' she said proudly, placing her immaculately manicured hand on his shoulder.

'So Vaugan has the cash to pay for communications advisers?' JBM asked quietly, turning the TV off with the remote.

'Apparently he has a large personal fortune,' said Domitile.

'A personal fortune? Are you kidding? His father was the local cobbler in Juvisy and his mother was a typist. He didn't have a sou to his name ...'

'How do you know that?' Domitile asked, surprised.

JBM shrugged.

'I must have read it at the barber's ...'

One of Domitile's assistants came to fetch her to discuss something to do with camera settings for the shoot at Gare de Lyon.

'Did you really know him?' asked Aurore.

'Yes. In another life, he was an exceptional bassist.'

'A bassist?'

'Yes, he played bass guitar in a rock band, a new-wave pop band; well, cold wave to be precise. Stan Lepelle, the artist, was in the band too. The guitarist is a doctor now, I think, like his father. I financed the demo tape, Pierre wrote the lyrics ... Sadly it didn't come to anything, but it was good. I've often told myself that group was my one real failure. The only thing I've backed that didn't work out.'

'Did you sing vocals for them?'

'No, not me. That was a woman.'

'What happened to her?'

'I don't know,' he mumbled. Then he went quiet.

'I'll go and see how they're getting on,' said Aurore, and she went off towards the garden.

JBM's gaze rested on the black leather bag that held Pierre's urn. He had gone to fetch it from the bank the day before. The previous week, he had stumbled on an article about the Désert de Retz, a once privately owned garden on the edge of the Forêt de Marly filled with bizarre and esoteric-looking structures, and it had seemed to match Pierre's wish to have his ashes scattered in a 'place of beauty and history'. What was more, Pierre had often talked about this mythical place, the last flight of fancy of a misanthropic aesthete aristocrat, unveiled just a few years before the French Revolution. JBM would head over there later that afternoon. The park-keeper had granted his request, despite the fact it was against the law to scatter ashes in a public park – JBM had offered a substantial donation towards the restoration of park buildings and upon handing over the cheque became a 'five-star friend' of the garden.

'Where do we go when we die, Pierre?' JBM whispered. He got no reply. 'Sometimes I can feel you near me, sense your presence and the smell of your cigars ... and sometimes I can't. Shit,' he mumbled, leaning forward on the sofa, 'why did you leave me? Send me a sign, anything ...'

Aurore took a step back, and then another. He hadn't noticed her come back into the living room. JBM smoothed back his hair and stared straight ahead. He sniffed, threw a cushion against the sofa in a fit of rage, and took several deep breaths. Aurore waited a few seconds and then knocked at the glass pane of the door. JBM turned round.

'Come in.'

His expression was almost calm.

'Shall we go then?' he said, getting to his feet and picking up the black leather bag as they headed out to the car.

'He's livid,' she whispered in his ear, nodding in the direction of Max, the driver.

Max was standing beside a Renault, arms crossed and chin raised, glaring at Domitile, who was on the phone. He took their bags – except for the one with Pierre's ashes, which JBM kept with him – placed them in the boot and snatched the Louis Vuitton handbag from Domitile as she handed it to him. Then he got behind the wheel and slammed his door shut. The 'confiscation', as he put it, of the Lincoln had been taken as a personal affront. Domitile had decided it would be a good idea if for the time being JBM swapped his American car for a French one. For the sake of a quiet life with Blanche, JBM had agreed to everything, though he fully intended to take the Lincoln back as soon as 'all the fuss' was over.

Le Train Bleu

The nicest and most cheering thing about Domitile was that everything was always 'amazing', 'fantastic', 'spot on'. People in comms must have been raised in special nurseries; they had surely been drip-fed transfusions of optimism and self-confidence from the moment they were born. Indeed, perhaps the very purpose of their job was to try to pass on this fabulous fluid to their clients. The whole time JBM had been standing on this platform at Gare de Lyon, Domitile had been as excitable as a small child. Placing him at the end of the platform and getting his picture taken seemed to please her as much as if she were a little girl opening a Barbie doll's house under the Christmas tree. She marched about in her stilettos, showering JBM with a stream of pointers as the shots flashed up on the preview screen: 'So handsome, amazing, spot on, look up a bit.'

'How long is this going to go on? We've got a lot of work to do,' said Aurore.

'Well, so have I,' replied Domitile. 'I'm working for France here.'

As she stopped and glanced at Aurore, who was staring at her blankly, she reminded herself that the young woman she was talking to was not a nobody, but someone who had taken up an entire page of the last issue of *Forbes* as part of its 'Tycoon's Angels' piece; she wasn't the work experience girl on photocopying duty, but a PA whom many of the world's top business people would happily poach for a six-figure salary.

'Yes, I understand,' she said, having got a grip on herself. 'Don't worry, Aurore. We'll just wait for the sun to come out again and then he's all yours.'

'Aurore!' JBM called after her. 'I don't know how long we're going to be pissing around for. Can I put you in charge for this morning? You've got everything with you, haven't you?'

'Everything, yes.'

'England, Russia?'

'Everything, yes,' she repeated.

'Perfect. You can get started then, while I'm ... play-acting on a station platform,' he moaned, heading back into position.

A quarter of an hour later, the light still wasn't good and they agreed to take a break. Sitting cross-legged at the foot of a pillar, Aurore had spread out in front of her two folders, three iPhones and two tablets and, stopping to put headphones in, had got out pen and paper and begun taking notes while talking to someone in Russian. JBM walked over to her.

'All OK?' he asked quietly.

'Everything's fine,' she whispered.

'I'm going to grab a coffee at Le Train Bleu. See you in there.'

Aurore nodded. The photographer came and sat next to Domitile, who was scrolling through the shots on the digital screen, and his gaze fell on Aurore.

'She's pretty. I'd like to take her picture – do you think she'd mind?'

'Don't even think about it,' Domitile replied without taking her eyes off the screen. 'Under no circumstances are you to approach her.'

*

JBM pushed the revolving door of the famous brasserie and a maître d' came straight over to greet him.

'I'd like to have a coffee.'

'A coffee ...' the maître d' echoed. 'I've got the little rooms off to the left here,' he said, visibly frustrated, 'but I'm going to find you something better.'

He clicked his fingers at a passing waiter.

'A coffee on table 12!' he instructed.

'Thanks,' mumbled JBM.

'You're welcome, Monsieur Mazart,' the maître d' replied with a smile.

JBM followed the waiter and sat at an empty table in the main dining room. At the surrounding tables, a couple were finishing their lunch, as were a quartet of businessmen who lowered their voices and did their best to hide the fact they were talking about him. A few tables back, a lone woman sat watching him with a slight smile on her lips. Resting her elbow on the tablecloth, she was cupping her chin in the palm of her hand. It seemed as if she might sit there for ages, contemplating JBM. He was looking back at her when suddenly his expression became one of astonishment. He mouthed, 'Bérengère?'

She slowly nodded her head as she made out her name on his lips. JBM pushed back his table, stood up and walked towards her.

The seven or so metres between them seemed like an ocean of time, a kind of uncertain limbo in which each step counted for several years. By the time he reached her table, thirty years would have flown by. Bérengère, who would for ever be twenty in the mind of JBM, now appeared before him in the body of a fifty-year-old woman.

'Hi, Jean,' she said as he stood before her. 'I missed my train,' she told him with a shrug, as if she felt the need to explain why she was there.

'Excuse me,' said the waiter, holding a tray. 'Will you be having your coffee at this table, Monsieur?'

JBM glanced at Bérengère and wavered for a moment: should he impose upon her, or have his coffee taken to his own table? Bérengère cut in, 'Put it here, please,' and JBM sat down.

The long fringe that used to fall over her eyes had gone, and she now wore her hair in a bob. Her face had changed, of course, but was in many ways still very similar to that of the girl of the 1980s. The veil of years had barely fallen over it, casting a very slight mist over the features she had once had. Those former features kept coming back to superimpose themselves on this new face, as though trying to fit – which they did pretty well, in fact – like geometric fractals seeking an anchor point before the equation is fixed. The look in her eyes was unchanged, with an ironic glint in their depths that seemed to say that life plays some awful tricks on us, and who knows what the future will hold, but it doesn't really matter after all. Judging by the few words she had spoken, her voice was still the same too – soft, slow, a touch serious. A voice he had not heard in thirty-three years.

'Well, this is a surprise,' said JBM.

'Yes.' Bérengère smiled and looked down at her coffee. 'Life's full of surprises.'

'You're still just as beautiful,' he added after a pause.

'You old charmer,' she murmured and looked up at him.

What do you say to the woman you were in love with more than thirty years ago when you bump into her at a train station? A woman you know you'll only spend a few minutes with, and never see again? It was like drawing a tarot card from a fortune teller, as if life had decided to do you a favour, not by offering a second chance, but by giving you a kind of knowing wink. Bérengère interrupted his thoughts.

'Well done,' she said, clinking her cup against his, 'for everything you've achieved in the last thirty years. But I always knew you'd do it.'

'Thanks,' mumbled JBM. 'How about you? What have you been up to?'

'Not quite as much as you have.' She smiled. 'I took over my parents' hotel.'

'Le Relais de la Clef?'

'You remember the name?' she asked, taken aback.

JBM nodded.

'Well, not a lot has changed in the last thirty years. The region is still making wine – the best in the world – the tourists still come and the Romanée-Conti is still just as expensive,' she laughed, running her hand through her hair.

JBM laughed along with her, but chose not to mention the memory that was coming back to him. When they spent the weekend there once, one of the winemakers from the prestigious estate that produced the most sought-after wine on the planet had offered each of them a glass, straight out of the vats. Ever since, despite having it offered to him several times, JBM had always politely refused to drink it, coming up with all kinds of excuses – he wanted the scent and taste of Romanée-Conti to remain for ever associated with the memory of Bérengère.

'Your parents ...' JBM asked cautiously.

'My father is no longer with us, and my mother moved to a retirement home in Beaune. What about yours?'

JBM shook his head.

'Are you married?' he went on.

'I was ... We separated, and he died five years ago.'

'I'm sorry.'

'I know you're married,' Bérengère carried on. 'Do you have kids?'

'Yes.'

JBM was finding it hard to shake the image of that sunny afternoon on the Romanée-Conti estate from his mind. It was an episode he had hardly ever thought about, but in the space of a few seconds it had come back strongly, almost violently, like a buried fossil brought shiny and whole from the ground. An afternoon in the early 1980s, when they were young and had, as the trite yet very true expression goes, their whole lives ahead of them. And life had flown by, like a letter in the post.

'Girl or boy?' Bérengère asked when he failed to elaborate.

'Boys,' said JBM, coming back down to earth. 'I have two sons. I never had a daughter,' he added with a note of regret.

Bérengère lowered her head slightly, still holding his gaze.

'You?'

'I have a daughter.'

'How old is she?'

'Thirty-three. How old are your sons?'

'Twenty-two and twenty-four.'

'Time flies ...'

'Yes,' murmured JBM. 'I can't believe I'm here with you.'

Bérengère nodded.

'What about Pierre? What's he up to these days?' she asked brightly.

'Pierre ... passed away last year.'

'I'm so sorry, Jean ...'

'It's fine.' He smiled sadly and added, 'I think it would have amused him to see us sitting here together. It's funny, I was talking about you barely a couple of hours ago – well, not you directly, but the songs.'

'It was a sign,' said Bérengère.

'Maybe,' JBM said softly. 'Maybe if you think about someone hard enough, you might just make them appear.'

'Were you thinking hard about me?' she asked in mock astonishment.

JBM smiled back at her, unsure of the most tactful way to reply. In the end he didn't have to: Bérengère's phone buzzed as a text message arrived. She turned it over, looked at the message briefly and put it down again as another one came through, swiftly followed by a third.

'You're in demand,' remarked JBM.

Bérengère nodded.

'You and I went to see a film,' he went on, 'at an arthouse cinema on Boulevard Saint-Michel, a black and white film which had a scene shot in here, at Le Train Bleu.'

'*La Maman et la Putain* by Jean Eustache, with Jean-Pierre Léaud, Bernadette Lafont and Françoise Lebrun.'

'That's the one.'

He closed his eyes for a few seconds, opened them again and, looking at Bérengère, lifted his finger and began to recite:

'"I like this place a lot. I come here when I'm feeling down. The people here are usually just passing through. It's like a Murnau film, always going from the city to the country, from day to night; it's the same here: on the right,"' said JBM, pointing to the revolving door leading out of the brasserie to the station, '"trains, the countryside ... On the left,"' he said, turning towards the windows, '"the city ..."'

He stopped talking.

'God,' Bérengère muttered solemnly, shaking her head. 'What an amazing memory ... Please tell me you've seen it again since?'

'No, never,' JBM replied almost sadly.

She closed her eyes and opened them again to look at her watch.

'I have to go. My train's already here.'

'I'll walk with you.'

'The light's fantastic,' said the photographer.

'We wanted it, we got it,' Domitile chipped in from behind the test screen.

'Head up, thank you. That's good. You seem a bit more tense than earlier,' the photographer remarked.

'Relax, JBM. You're terrific, imperial,' boomed Domitile.

'The Emperor died on St Helena, Domitile, and he didn't die of poisoning, as some people say. He died of boredom,' replied JBM, holding his pose.

'Well, that won't happen to you,' retorted Domitile. 'Look up a bit – perfect!'

Even more than the emotions that had been churned up by seeing Bérengère again – emotions he couldn't share with anybody – something about this brief encounter was niggling him, as if he had missed something.

Bérengère

It's easy to forget people, faces, names. I don't have a clear picture of Alain, for example, the guitarist in our band, who was studying medicine and whose father was also a doctor. When the time came to send off the demo tape, we had to give an address in case the record company wanted to call us in. Putting down five different addresses seemed likely to cause confusion, so we stuck to one: if a letter arrived, the person who received it would let the others know. Vaugan, living out in Juvisy, warned us that post in his area often went missing; JBM was renting a studio but didn't intend to stay long, and was thinking of moving to live in a hotel all year round. His brother was living with a woman but they were on the verge of splitting up; Lepelle was sharing an art studio-cum-flat with other students from the École des Beaux-Arts, and I was on strained terms with my landlord, who thought I had too many visitors to my attic room. Alain's address – an apartment block in the eighth *arrondissement* whose lobby could be accessed without an entry code during the day because Alain's father was a doctor who received patients there – seemed the best idea, especially as there was a new Portuguese concierge who could be relied upon to distribute the mail conscientiously. But no letter ever came.

Even if I close my eyes and try to summon his face, I can't

quite see it – it's like a name on the tip of my tongue. Alain had brown hair, cut in a mullet. I think he liked me, but I was going out with JBM, so he couldn't do anything about it. He gave me a forty-five of 'Les Mots Bleus' by Christophe. He loved the song and claimed it had kicked off the new-wave movement – an opinion none of the rest of us shared. Having since heard it countless times on the radio and on TV, I've ended up coming round to his view – there was something pure and cold, something deeply purposeful about Christophe's song, which was ahead of its time. Maybe it was just a present after all, maybe Alain never did have feelings for me. It was all so long ago.

Another face has slipped out of my memory – the boy who played the synth. I can't picture him at all, not even an outline; all I know is I think his hair was blond or mousy; even his name escapes me. I do remember Stan Lepelle – who at the time wasn't Stan but Stanislas. I've seen his face many times since, most recently only a week ago in an article in *Le Monde* about his giant brain installation in the Tuileries. He's changed a lot – now he has his hair short, but it used to be very curly, and he'd wear leather cuffs around his wrists. I would never have dreamt he would make a career in modern art. He used to say he had only gone to the Beaux-Arts to keep his parents happy – better for him to go to art school after his baccalaureate than hang around making music. He was good at art, but it wasn't what he was really interested in. His thing was drums – he knew the names of all the great rock drummers by heart, and went as far as to question how talented the Stones drummer Charlie Watts really was. If there was one person out of all of us I thought would make a career in music, it was him. Him and Vaugan, of course. Vaugan was overweight at the time, with a chubby baby face accentuated by his pudding-basin haircut. He was quite a shy boy. He kept to himself.

It wasn't until twenty-five years later that I happened to catch a late-night TV programme, saw a man with a shaved head, heard the presenter say his name, and caught something in his eyes that convinced me it wasn't someone else who shared his name: the divisive character in a black T-shirt and Sébastien from Juvisy really were one and the same person.

When we were in the band, I knew he had a thing for a girl who lived on his road whom he often saw at the bus stop in Juvisy. He didn't have the courage to speak to her, and vaguely told me about her while looking down at his shoes. Once I walked back to his parents' place with him, and he whispered, 'That's her,' as a pretty blonde girl passed us on the pavement. 'Hi, Séb,' she said. 'Hi, Nathalie,' Vaugan replied. 'Talk to her – now's the time,' I urged him, but he shook his head and grumbled something he didn't mean me to understand. Whatever happened to that girl, with her plaited blonde hair? Does she still remember Vaugan? Maybe not. Has she made the link between her old neighbour, fat Séb with the bowl-cut hair who played the bass, and the man now calling for France to pull out of the European pact and send all foreigners home? Fat Séb is probably nothing more than a blurry shadow from her past, a walk-on part without any lines, whom the camera never even focuses on; he passes through the back of the shot, a hazy, elusive figure.

'Pierre passed away.' 'I'm so sorry,' I replied. I saw Pierre once, strangely enough at Gare de Lyon. He was holding a painting that was all wrapped up, and was looking a bit flustered as he made his way out to the taxi rank, shouting 'Mind your backs!' to clear a path like a waiter in a restaurant. It made me smile. I didn't say anything; he was already a long way away. That must have been a good twenty years ago. Pierre was a regular at parties thrown by art history students from the École du Louvre. Most of them were girls, and many came from very wealthy families and were already living in lovely studio flats paid for by their parents. We looked up to Pierre – he seemed just as knowledgeable as our lecturers but was much younger than them – not yet thirty. He fell into an age bracket somewhere between us and our teachers, and we of course saw him as one of us. He was very eccentric, with his pocket watch and his cravats. One evening he brought his younger brother along to a party in a little flat on Rue Jacob. That's how I met JBM. He asked to listen to our songs. I had a tape in my Walkman (with orange-foam-covered headphones) and went to get it out of my bag. He listened to the songs without saying anything; he just looked at me and slowly sipped his vodka. As the cassette played, I found myself unable to pull away from him. I was nineteen, he was twenty-three.

'It's very good,' he said, taking the headphones off. 'I really like it, but I think it could be better. You need to record it in a proper studio to get the sound quality right. Also, one of the songs has a really nice tune, but the words are a bit bland ...'

'You can write us some new ones then,' I laughed – I wasn't sure if he was taking our songs seriously or if we were really only flirting.

'No, I wouldn't know where to start,' he said with a smile, 'but Pierre might have some ideas. He's written poems ... Pierre!' He called his brother over. And that's how it all began.

'Your song's amazing,' I told Pierre when he gave us his lyrics. 'I didn't write the chorus, though,' he said modestly. 'It's Shakespeare.' There was a spoken section that also wasn't his;

he had adapted it from *Le Grand Meaulnes* by Alain-Fournier. I might not have JBM's memory, but I can still remember it: 'This is happiness, this is what you spent your whole youth looking for, this is the girl you saw at the end of all your dreams!' It was very hard to pronounce. There was a trend at the time for songs in English. There was something about that track. I don't know why it didn't work out. I never had any regrets, either about the album or my year at the École du Louvre, that I failed by a whisker.

With no university place and no JBM, there no longer seemed to be much reason to stay in Paris. I went back to Burgundy and my future seemed to be laid out for me – or so I thought. Whenever I think about that time I find myself coming back to him; I hadn't seen Jean for thirty-three years – counting it up like that, it's almost impossible to believe. Though I hadn't seen him 'in real life', he was never out of my thoughts, and I was always hearing other people talk about him.

It's all so long ago, images are coming back into my head like photos you find in a shoebox at the bottom of the cupboard, images that represent your childhood or youth and whose only value is as evidence to prove you really were there, at that time, surrounded by those people. A moment fixed on paper, of which nothing now remains. You never went back to that place, or it has changed beyond recognition; people have gone their separate ways and you've lost touch, or they've died, and you yourself no longer have the face you once had. It all belonged to another life. Thinking about all this, I don't know whether to laugh or cry.

Jean said he wanted to go back to the States for a year or two, get back in touch with some people he knew at MIT. I couldn't imagine leaving everything behind to follow him: what would I do in the United States? I knew what his departure meant: the end of our relationship. I knew too that I couldn't stop him from going, that nothing would ever hold him back; I almost managed to console myself by thinking I had been lucky to have him for a little while. Our relationship lasted a little over a year, 409 days to be precise – I counted once, when I came across my old diaries. I had written 'Jean' and drawn a heart for the day we met, and 409 days later, in a new diary, were the words 'Jean left'. Then I met François and everything happened very quickly; I agreed straight away when he asked me to marry him. I threw myself into it in order to put Jean behind me. The truth is that seeing him has really thrown me. I feel like having a good cry but the tears aren't coming; I'm crying inside, as my mother used to say. How could fate have been so cruel to us? And so inclined to play tricks.

U-turn

Torrential rain was hitting the windscreen, and the driver had set the wipers going, squeaking slightly as they moved in time with one another. The magical light Domitile had kept on talking about had vanished the moment the photo shoot on the platform ended. She had already emailed four photos to Aurore to get JBM's feedback while she worked on a second selection made up of pictures taken in the garden with Blanche and the ones from the kitchen, which she was already describing as 'imbued with immense desirability'.

Aurore scrolled through the four pictures from the station. Total pain in the arse she might be, but credit where credit was due: Domitile had managed to get the best shot of JBM that Aurore had ever seen. The train tracks faded into a kind of haze that merged with the sky; JBM was standing tall – the photographer had centred him in a 'chest shot'; his grey jacket hung perfectly; the white shirt, with just the top button undone, was chic; he was looking into the distance, a half-smile on his lips; and the ever-present hint of irony in his eyes was barely noticeable. The first three shots were almost identical. The fourth had caught him mid-movement: looking upwards, JBM was running his left hand through his hair as a gust of wind swept through the station. The Breguet chronometer watch was hidden, but you got a good view of the smart cufflinks.

Caught mid-gesture, his hand was slightly out of focus, which gave a sense of movement to the picture – something Domitile underlined in her email, while adding that, in her opinion, they should choose from the pictures showing static poses. When Aurore suggested that JBM look through the pictures on his iPad, he shook his head gently and began staring out at the city in the rain. He hadn't said a word since they got in the car, but sat looking out at the crossroads and passers-by at red lights, without appearing to really see them.

'I never had a daughter. You?' 'I have a daughter.' 'How old is she?' 'Thirty-three. How old are your sons?' 'Twenty-two and twenty-four.' 'Time flies ...'

It was there. JBM was replaying the brief exchange in his mind. Something had happened then. Something he had not been conscious of, but which his brain had picked up on. It had only lasted a moment, and now he would swear it was between the first sentence, 'I never had a daughter,' and the next, when he had thrown the question back at Bérengère: 'You?' Something had come about in those two seconds. Maybe no more than one second. It was absolutely infinitesimal, like subliminal images slipped into a film sequence that the brain grasps but the eye doesn't see. JBM concentrated and tried to rid his mind of extraneous detail, the decor of the brasserie, the murmur of conversations and the sounds of cutlery. He was getting closer to it. There had been a faint hint of something on Bérengère's lips and the look in her eyes had intensified. He could tell he almost had it when finally the image slipped anchor and rose up to the surface: the merest trace of irony had flitted across her mouth and come across in her expression. During their brief reunion, there had been surprise, awkwardness, nostalgia, tenderness and even a little sadness, but not *irony* – or only at that split second. 'I never had a daughter.' So it was to this statement that Bérengère had replied with an ironic smile. Thirty-three. If that was how old she was now, Bérengère must have had a child just after they split up. There was a wide spectrum of dates within which the child's birth could have fallen. Bérengère might have met someone else and fallen pregnant very soon after their break-up. In which case, why that smile? There was nothing to justify it. I didn't say anything 'funny', mused JBM. But no sooner had he had this thought, than it occurred to him that the opposite might be true: I said I didn't have a daughter, and there's only one person in the world who could smile *ironically* at that statement.

'Max, how long does it take to get to Dijon by car?'

'Dijon ... I'd say three and a half hours. Less than four, anyway.'

'And by TGV?' he asked Aurore.

'An hour and a half, isn't it?' the driver hazarded, seeking Aurore's approval in the rear-view mirror.

'Something like that,' she said.

'Do a U-turn; we're going back to the station. Book us two tickets, please, Aurore; we can work on the train.'

'But ... what are we going to Dijon for? Can't it wait?' she asked, stunned. 'What about the Désert de Retz? What about Pierre?'

'No, it can't wait. Pierre can come with us for now.'

Aurore turned to her phone.

'There's a train in fourteen minutes,' she told them.

'Max,' JBM said soberly.

'We'll catch that one, Monsieur.' The driver switched into the bus lane and raced up it.

'What are we going to Dijon for?' Aurore asked again.

'We're not going to Dijon,' JBM replied. 'We're going to a place thirty kilometres outside it, between Vosne-Romanée and Nuits-Saint-Georges.'

The Man Who Would Play Drums

Feline and stoned. That would be Alain's abiding image of her. Lying on the sofa in denim shorts and white crop top, she had extended her long legs so that her bare feet rested on the arm and she was smoking a perfectly conical joint. Her hair was bizarrely arranged in a sort of palm tree and her languid gaze never left him. 'Ivana, a Russian artist,' was how Lepelle had introduced her. She was clearly his girlfriend – or mistress, but that came to the same thing. Alain wondered how a guy like Lepelle could have pulled such a beautiful girl – and so young at that. Some girls inspired poetry, songs, novels or pictures. This girl inspired something very complex, something between violation and a marriage proposal. For the second of those, the discovery of Ivana had come much too late in his life; and as for the first, it had never so much as crossed his mind to impose anything at all on a woman by force. Ivana, for that was her name, would for ever remain languidly on her sofa, perfectly inaccessible, in the manner of those fabulous fish that you gaze at through thick glass in an aquarium. Like them, she barely communicated with her visitors and seemed to inhabit her own world, which Alain imagined full of snow, lovers, contraband vodka and wolves.

Lepelle had not particularly wanted to see Alain, but he had let himself be talked into it. In the beginning, Alain had frequently come to his performances, notably the pencil-sharpening. The last time they had met was back in 2000, when the Cartier Foundation had mounted a little retrospective devoted to the *matiéristes*, the movement that had launched Lepelle at the beginning of the 1990s. He had sent him an invitation for the opening, but they hadn't really had a chance to talk at the party.

'It's lucky that your letter never arrived,' said Lepelle vehemently, handing back Polydor's missive which he had just read after putting on the half-moon spectacles that he now removed. 'Imagine where we would be now ...'

Alain was wondering what he meant and Ivana was waving her hand so that she too could read the letter. Alain passed it over, along with the envelope.

'You live on Rue de Moscou?' she said, astonished. 'There's a Moscow Street here?'

'Yes, and just beside it, there's Rue Saint-Pétersbourg. It changed its name; before it was Rue de Leningrad.'

'Is it the Russian quarter?' she asked in her thick accent.

'No, the European quarter; all the streets are named after a capital city, or a major city.'

'We'd have been pitiful has-beens, that's what we would have been,' resumed Lepelle, getting up from his armchair. 'We'd have been fifty-somethings scraping a living between unemployment benefit and gigs at suburban youth clubs for eighty euros a time. A life of nothingness, a life of failure, that's what we've been saved from by your letter being lost in the post. You should send flowers to your postman.'

Alain had not known what to expect at the meeting Lepelle had organised at his home-studio in Yvelines, but it certainly was not this. 'We might also have been successful,' he objected. 'Plenty of groups made it, look at Téléphone—'

'Téléphone broke up,' cut in Lepelle, 'and a long time ago. Anyway, Téléphone was way before us, in 1977, before wave; they were punk rock, Téléphone.'

'What difference does it make if Téléphone aren't together any more?' retorted Alain. 'Depeche Mode, the Eurythmics, The Cure were all famous for a while – that's what counts, isn't it? And Indochine still exists.'

'Wrong.' Lepelle's tone was brisk. 'Indochine got back together, that's different. And it's only because Nicola Sirkis is a nutcase, obsessed with his own glory and he needs Indochine. I recognise that he was very courageous in the wilderness years, all of the nineties. He continued to believe in himself, when everyone had forgotten him … No, frankly, look at you, a GP; you live well; all your patients' illnesses pay for your country house, if you have one, your children's education, good restaurants, holidays … Even Vaugan was right to give up on the band, and JBM too. You think he would have been fulfilled as our producer, our manager? No, JBM had another destiny and he knew it. And our singer, Bérengère, what became of her? No one knows. As for me? Eh? Me? Don't you think I prefer being what I am, rather than a lame drummer chasing recognition at provincial festivals? I'm rich and famous, a celebrity even, and with the band all I would have been was a loser along with all of you.'

'You are a loser,' said Ivana, exhaling the smoke from her joint.

'Give that back,' Lepelle snapped, snatching the letter from her and handing it over to Alain, who put it back in the envelope.

'OK, well, did you keep the tape or not?'

Lepelle sighed and shrugged. 'Do you really think, my poor old friend, I would have kept that for thirty-three years? And what about you, do you still have the pencil shavings? You know, they'll be worth a lot; you made a good investment. How much did you pay for them?'

'I can't remember,' replied Alain. 'It was still francs then – a thousand francs, I think.'

'There you go then!' cried Lepelle. 'Today, old chap, they're worth twenty thousand euros. Oh yes,' nodding his head as if he had just bestowed manna from heaven and Alain should be very honoured.

Alain finished his glass of orange juice. His quest was useless – those he could reach no longer had the cassette. What had he succeeded in tracking down? A megalomaniac fascist in the grip of political madness, a man with a boil from a Thai resort – at this hour he would be tucking in to one of his favourite grilled fish with a flower on top – and today an arrogant contemporary artist, proud of his success and contemptuous of the Holograms.

Some days earlier, before Lepelle had deigned to make contact with him, Alain had reread Polydor's letter and had suddenly wondered about its author: Claude Kalan, artistic director. The internet had provided some information about the producer, now retired. He seemed to have had his heyday in the 1980s and 1990s. He must have been one of those quiet people whose name no one knows, but whose work is familiar to everyone. One of those people who, without giving any sign of it, have amassed a large fortune by producing records that everybody recognises. Alain found several Top 50 hits under his name, along with collaborations with famous artists, French as well as foreign. Google Images, on the other hand, only had two recent photos, both very small and taken from a long way away. They showed a slight man with white hair, who must have been about seventy. Alain had scanned the Polydor letter, and started to write back, thirty-three years after the man had requested a meeting.

He explained that the postal service had lost the letter, of which he enclosed a copy, and asked him, without any great hope, whether he remembered the Holograms. He did not bother asking whether Polydor or Kalan had kept the five-track cassette. He had really only written to Kalan as a sort of confession, to talk to someone about it and to tell the story. Then he had telephoned the record company where a young girl had confirmed that Monsieur Kalan had retired but that Alain could send his letter to the company and they would ensure that it was sent on. But Kalan had not replied yet and probably never would.

It was very quiet. Alain watched the flames behind the heat-resistant glass of the fireplace. The room was high-ceilinged, painted entirely white and opened on to an American-style kitchen. A little further away, through a very large window, you could see the studio and the garden. Although the overall impression was cold and soulless, Alain knew that this place was worth at least two million euros, maybe three. Alain had no desire to prolong the encounter. In the end, Lepelle was right. He had a comfortable life, and the best place for the letter was the waste-paper basket. He took his leave.

No sooner had Lepelle closed the door behind him than Ivana had remonstrated with him. 'Why don't you give him his songs? You really are a horrible man.'

Lepelle did not bother to reply. He sat down heavily in a

141

chair, as if stunned, his eyes staring, muttering curses. Then the muttering became a crescendo until he got to his feet and yelled, 'Damn it to hell, we would have made it!' He repeated, 'We would have made it! I knew we were good!' He was shouting and flinging his arms up as if he were addressing God. 'I knew it, I always knew it.' He groaned. 'And as for that bastard who came to show me his letter!' In his fury, he picked up a magazine and hurled it at the door. 'It's too much to bear. That would have meant everything to me, everything! When will this ever end?'

And he picked up another magazine, tore it to shreds and threw them around the room.

Ivana

The room with all the records is at the other end of the house. It's so big that you have to stand on a sliding ladder to get to the top shelves. Lepelle has thousands of records, thirty-threes and forty-fives, and thousands of CDs and audio tapes too. The guy has the whole history of rock, pop, disco and new wave. In the middle of the room is his drum kit with Tama written on the side of the bass drum. He says it's the best brand of drums in the world. There's also a sound system with enormous speakers that he had put on specially made slate stands to make the sound better. He shuts himself in there and spends hours going for it on the drums. When the room's empty, I'm allowed to go in there and listen to whatever I want, as long as I put the records back in the right order and don't copy anything.

On one of the shelves, there are some framed pictures of him looking young and holding his drumsticks, and on the same shelf there are the records and audio tapes he helped to make, about ten of them. To begin with, he didn't want me to listen to them, but then he was happy for me to. No doubt about it, Lepelle was a good, maybe even very good, drummer. On the same shelf, there's the Holograms cassette with the black and white photo of the group and the song 'Such Stuff as Dreams Are Made On'. What I think is that the record room is like a mausoleum for his own dreams. I told him that once and he just looked at me. I think the truth is he has never got over not having made it in the music business. Playing drums in recording studios, concert halls, being on the road, jumping on groupies in hotel rooms, leaving again the next day and doing the same thing over and over until the end of the tour, when he would lock himself away with his hi-hat and drums – that would have been the ideal life for him. Lepelle would have been 'cool' and happy as a musician; modern art has never brought him the fame he wanted and now he's 'bitter'. That's a word I only learnt recently, and I think it suits him. It means you're going round in circles like a snake in a basket, exactly like he does; he's jealous of all the artists with a bigger following than him. He spends his time inventing enemies, like he has an obsession with a collector of French contemporary art who hasn't bought any of his work; he even pinned a picture of this guy on the wall of his studio and throws darts at it. He's actually nothing like an artist; I think he's more like a village shopkeeper, the kind that spend their time plotting ways to steal customers off their competitors down the road.

Since he left, I have not stopped thinking about the grey-haired doctor who lives in a road that reminds me of Russia. Sometimes weed makes things foggy; everything becomes hazy and vague and faces don't stay in my head, but other times the drug has the power to fix them in my memory – the image is printed there like a photo.

I ask myself what I'm doing on this sofa, in this room, with this maniac I don't really know any better than the guys who ride me during a video shoot or a night in their hotel suite. I ask myself what I'm doing here and if, in the end, this isn't all just a dream: I'm going to wake up in my childhood bedroom and my father will take me out on his boat, then we'll come back for lunch and my mother will have made a piping-hot meal in the copper pot. Nothing happened; no casting director came to the village; no girl agreed to a photo shoot; Yuleva doesn't have a scar on her cheek, and I never lit my first joint with Sergei in Moscow. That night never turned into an orgy; no one filmed it and showed it to a Russian porn producer; I never said, 'OK, fine, let's do it,' to acting in films for three times what I was getting as a hostess; I never met the Frenchman looking for girls to film in France. I never left Russia for Paris and then this place called 'Yvelines' – to begin with I thought it was a girl's name. Nothing happened. Only one thing came about in my dream: I met the doctor with the grey hair who lives on Rue de Moscou.

I look at Lepelle; he's still ranting to himself about the meeting he missed. He can't stop; he's gone all red in the face. He turns to me and shouts, 'We had it; we would have made it as a rock band, and I wouldn't be sitting here making giant shoe studs for Qatar!' I watch him pick up the poker – I'm afraid he'll actually go mad and hit me with it, but instead he runs off towards his studio. I get up and walk towards the bay window. The big cast for the shoe stud is in pieces and there is loads of plaster dust floating in the air. Now I see him attacking his paint pots with the poker; the paint is splashing everywhere and he's covered in colours up to his hair. I tell myself, 'Ivana, my girl, that's enough now; it's time for you to go.' I will go, now, right away. I'll go up to my room and pack my bags. In a brown envelope hidden in my underwear drawer, I have more than twelve thousand euros; I can pay for all the hotel rooms I want, and plane tickets too. As for the songs he's going crazy over, that he won't even copy for his old friend, he can keep them and imagine they're his secret – I've already downloaded them onto my iPod.

Le Relais de la Clef

Two hours later, the taxi was pulling up outside Le Relais de la Clef. JBM paid the fare and got out first. He went up to the entrance, where there was an arbour and a courtyard leading in from the road, with a well in the middle of it.

'I'll leave you here,' said Aurore. 'I'll wait for you in that café.'

And she walked off with their laptop cases slung over her shoulders, towards the PMU sports bar on the corner.

'Yes, thanks, Aurore,' murmured JBM.

He stayed where he was, lost in memories of the past. He had not set foot here since the summer of 1983. Nothing had changed, not the arbour, courtyard, or well. It was totally surreal to be there. The round white cast-iron table was still in the same place, and he felt as if he might see the two of them sitting there, having a coffee before going for a walk among the vines. Actually physically being back in a place he had sometimes returned to in his mind made him feel as if the space-time continuum had suddenly been squeezed. As if it had all happened just now, or no more than a month ago, and not thirty-three years earlier.

He walked through the courtyard and opened the door to the hotel. The bell rang; he had forgotten about that. The entrance hall, with its tiled floor and oak-beamed ceiling, was exactly as it had been, as was the reception desk, if you didn't count the flat-screen computer that now had pride of place. There was the same smell of furniture polish in the air. The fabric lining the walls must have been replaced; it was more beige than terracotta in his memory of it. There was no one around. JBM stepped towards a wall-mounted display case, which showed off Bérengère's father's collection of mechanical corkscrews, carefully laid out top to tail. Then he went into the lounge – silent but for the crackling of logs on the fire. Nothing, or almost nothing, had changed in here either: the beautiful round table with the inlaid chessboard in the middle still stood between the two windows which looked out over the vineyard; there was even a game in progress. How many matches had been played on it since he was last here – hundreds? Thousands? Maybe fewer – some games could go on for ages. JBM thought back to the time he had been to see the famous lawyer Jacques Vergès at his mansion on Rue de Vintimille in Paris. There were lots of chess games laid out on different tables in his office-cum-library. The lawyer had games going with several 'penfriends', mostly based abroad, who would send instructions by fax or email for their next move, playing across borders. According to the master of the house, some of the matches had been going on for several years.

As he gazed at the chessboard, JBM realised one of the kings was in check – but no one had yet played or noticed the move. He went back out to the entrance hall. Bérengère was standing behind the desk, and she looked up at him.

Now they were sitting opposite one another at the big kitchen table. JBM had not touched his wine. The cookers were all switched off and the staff would not be back for several hours.

It was the calmest point of the afternoon; in any case, there were very few guests at this time of year.

'You said there was something you wanted to ask me ...'

'Yes, I have a question,' said JBM, staring into his glass.

Then he retreated into silence, and all that could be heard was the sound of the pendulum marking the seconds ticking by. JBM felt he could stay like this for hours, cradled by the sound of the clock, with a glass of wine in front of him and Bérengère looking at him.

'I can't ...' he eventually said.

'Why not?' Bérengère asked gently, but got no reply. 'Jean ...' she murmured, and it occurred to JBM that nobody called him that any more. His brother had been the only one, and he was gone.

'Bérengère,' he finally said, fixing his gaze on hers, 'did we have a child together?'

Bérengère stared back at him before lowering her head and letting her eyes fall distractedly on the breadcrumbs she was rolling into balls between her fingers.

'I don't think I can do this,' she said, shaking her head.

'Do what?'

'Lie ... I can manage not to tell the truth, but I just can't bring myself to lie. I don't know how to do it. I couldn't lie to her either,' she murmured. Then she looked up at him. 'You see, Jean, I'm not scared any more. No, that's not it,' she corrected herself. 'Actually you could say I'm so scared that I've stopped being scared. So, yes, the answer is yes. We had a child together, a daughter.'

With shining eyes, she sniffed briefly, smiled and shook her head, as if to say she was sorry for the tears that came and would not fall. JBM placed his hand over hers, but she pulled it away, apologising.

'Would it be possible ... for me to get to know her? To see her one day?' asked JBM.

Bérengère smiled, closed her eyes as if nothing mattered any more, and breathed in.

'You see, the thing is, Jean,' she said, looking up at him, 'you already know her; you see her every day. Our daughter's name is Aurore.'

Le Train Bleu (2)

The anxiety had begun to build that morning, low-level at first. The night before, Aurore had had dinner with her mother, as she usually did when she was in town. Domitile Kavanski and this Gare de Lyon photo-shoot business had come at the worst possible time: Bérengère's train to Dijon would be leaving while the PR team and JBM were at the station. She had kept on looking at her watch while the shots were being set up. When Bérengère's scheduled departure time finally arrived, she began to relax. Nothing had happened – the twisted quirk of fate that might have caused JBM and Bérengère to bump into one another had not come about.

When she had pushed open the door of Le Train Bleu to join him, something had shifted in the very order of things. The sky had come at least ten metres closer to the earth. She spotted him straight away, sitting with his back to her, opposite Bérengère. They were talking. The maitre d' had come towards her and asked her a question she didn't hear. She rushed back out of the brasserie. As she emerged from the revolving doors, the noise hit her. The station, people, trains. A fast-paced life run to timetables, meetings, projects – a life that carried on, when as far as she was concerned everything had just stopped. She leant against the wall and tried to think things through clearly. Bérengère had missed her train. That's what it had taken – for her to miss her train and go to Le Train Bleu for a coffee while she waited for the next one. For him to take a break from the damned photo shoot that seemed never-ending and also make his way to Le Train Bleu, to choose a table not far from hers and for the eyes of one to settle on the other. Aurore fought back a sob of rage and childishly stamped her heels twice. Then she took out her phone and sent her mother a text: 'Don't talk to him!' She realised straight away she was losing it; it was ridiculous, they were already talking. She followed up swiftly with another text to clarify things: 'Don't tell him anything!' adding, 'Call me afterwards!' But Bérengère had not called. What on earth had she said or done to make JBM decide to drop everything and head to Burgundy? He had worked something out, something significant enough to throw out all of his plans for the rest of the day.

What could a man and woman who hadn't seen each other for thirty years have talked about? Their lives and their children, obviously. She must have said something to give herself away, a date, or maybe her name. But no, he wouldn't have brought her with him if he had understood; he'd have gone alone. So he hadn't worked it out. Aurore felt as if her head might explode.

'Hi, sweetie, you all right?' asked the café owner, leaning down to kiss her on both cheeks. 'Here for a few days, are you?'

'No, just passing through. I thought I'd stop for a coffee.'

'I'll bring it over. Don't you want it inside? It's a bit cold out here.'

'No, I'm fine; it's nice to get some fresh air,' she replied, forcing a smile.

It was when he had asked Max how long it would take to get to Dijon that she knew something was afoot. As usual, Aurore had reserved a group of four seats to give them some peace and quiet. But the journey would be anything but peaceful. Not having wanted to leave the leather bag containing Pierre's ashes with the driver, JBM had placed it on the seat next to him and they had opened their laptops and started to work on the report of the calls Aurore had made to England and Russia during the shoot. Aurore wasn't following what JBM was saying; while he was speaking, she had tried to text her mother but couldn't get any reception. There was nothing more she could do, no influence she could have on the course of events.

After making JBM repeat a figure twice in a row, she asked to take a break and went and shut herself in the toilet, realising she was shaking. She forced herself to close her eyes and take deep breaths, but nothing helped. Was this what they called a panic attack? She had read on the internet that at the peak of a panic attack, you might experience a 'sense of impending death'. She couldn't stop shaking; the speed of the train was making it worse, and the confined space, in addition to a sudden loss of hearing, heightened her anxiety still further. Aurore carried on trying to breathe calmly while avoiding her reflection in the mirror; the image she had briefly caught was of a young blonde woman with a crazed look in her eyes and an unhealthily pale colour. Someone knocked loudly at the door, grumbling, 'There's a queue!' 'Shut up! Go away!' she shouted back before a wave of dizziness made her clutch the hand-drier to stop herself from falling. 'I need sugar,' she told herself out loud, 'that's it, sugar, and fast ...' She yanked open the door and marched off in the direction of the buffet car. She made her way up through the carriages, struggling against the train's momentum which threw her off balance and forced her several times to hold on to the nearest headrest. She pushed her way authoritatively to the front of the queue and interrupted the barman while he was taking someone else's order.

'I need sugar, please, right now; I'm having a hypo; I'm going to faint.'

The barman immediately abandoned his other customer, ran Aurore a glass of water, tore open several sachets of sugar and tipped their contents into the glass, stirred the liquid with a spoon and handed it to her. He didn't take his eyes off her until she had drained the glass. It was unthinkable that a passenger should fall ill in his bar; he had long prayed he would never have to open the defibrillator attached to the wall in case someone suffered a heart attack; he had been shown how to use it on a training course months before, but knew there was no way he would be able to put the theory into practice in a real emergency.

'You're very pale,' JBM said on her return.

Aurore told him she was fine; it must have been a 'spasm'.

'A spasm?' mumbled JBM. Neither of them seemed very convinced of this, nor quite sure what a spasm was.

'Let's stop working,' he said. 'Have a rest, have a nap.'

Aurore tried to protest but soon gave in. She settled into her seat, leaning towards the window; JBM lay his coat over her and she fell fast asleep.

Above the vines, the sky, scattered with the mauve clouds that mean fog in the morning, was taking on the orangey glow of the end of the day. Aurore knew there was no way her mother could do it. She would never manage to keep the truth from JBM when he was standing in front of her. It was a question of minutes, she told herself as she stared over at the entrance to Le Relais de la Clef. She had watched him go inside; he would have found Bérengère by now. Soon he would know everything. The secret that had been kept nearly all her life would come crashing down in a matter of seconds, like shares in decades-old companies that seemed solid as a rock and then vanish into thin air in the space of a morning of panic on the stock markets. The waiter brought her coffee and Aurore poured in the sugar and slowly turned the spoon.

Aurore

It all happened at Clos Vougeot, the legendary Burgundy chateau that's like a ship sailing through the vines: that's where my parents met at a 'chapter' of the Chevaliers du Tastevin and where, fifteen years later, at another chapter, all was revealed. What a fitting word, chapter: the story of my life is written in them, and that of the gatherings of the association of Burgundy wine lovers that go by the same name, during which new members are sworn in at a ceremony with masonic undertones and then hundreds of guests of all nationalities sit down to a banquet to celebrate.

In the first chapter, my mother met François Delfer, Asia sales manager of the Bouchard winery. In the second, I had a brief conversation with an elderly man – a chevalier emeritus of the Confrérie, he wore a silver tastevin cup on a yellow and red ribbon around his neck. He motioned for me to come over to where he stood in the courtyard of the chateau.

'I'm told you're Bérengère Leroy's daughter.'

'That's me,' I replied.

'Remind me, what's your name?'

'Aurore.'

'That's right, Aurore ... Aurore,' he said proudly, raising his finger. 'You were my last child.'

I still remember my surprise, how I replied with a polite

'Pardon?' that must have betrayed my astonishment.

'I'm Dr Lessart. I delivered you shortly before I retired. Where is your mother? I'd very much like to see her. I was a regular at Le Relais de la Clef, way back when – the restaurant, I mean, of course; my wife and I used to go there quite a lot, and I knew your grandparents well too.'

I turned round and scoured the little groups of people gathered about the courtyard, waiters weaving between them holding silver trays laden with glasses of *crémant*, but I couldn't see Maman.

'I'm not sure. She must be around here somewhere ... I was premature, wasn't I?' I said in order to keep up the conversation with a man old enough to be my grandfather.

'Oh, no.' The doctor shook his head. 'You were born right on cue, my dear.'

He drained his glass of *crémant* and added, 'It's hard to remember every single child, but the first and the last do stick in the mind.'

I was about to reply when a group dressed in traditional hunting gear started playing the undulating tune known as 'Le Vol ce l'est' on their horns. Someone called Dr Lessart over. Before walking away, he placed his hand affectionately on my head and said, loudly over the sound of the brass instruments, 'Tell your mother I'm here, Aurore.' The resounding melody that can often be heard echoing through the forests, and that had until then always made me think of the animals that were about to die, went on, rousing and solemn in the chateau's courtyard. From then on, I would always associate the sound with that moment in my life.

'Was I a premature baby?' I asked my mother the next

day, while we were folding the sheets together in one of the bedrooms.

'Yes,' Bérengère replied matter-of-factly.

'How premature?'

'Three weeks.'

'The doctor who delivered me said I wasn't born prematurely but exactly when I was due.'

'Dr Lessart? Where did you see Dr Lessart?'

'At Vougeot last night. He came over to talk to me.'

'And you didn't say anything?'

'I couldn't find you, and then I lost him. There were six hundred people there.'

'And he said you weren't premature? He's forgotten,' my mother said, avoiding my eye.

But I wouldn't leave it there. I could tell she was hiding something.

'He remembers me very clearly. He said I was the last baby he delivered before he retired. He remembers you too. Apparently he used to come here all the time with his wife.'

My mother shrugged.

'Lots of people have been here, Aurore. Can you just help me with the sheets?'

We carried on the parallel dance, stepping towards each other and away again, holding the corners of the sheets tightly between our fingers until they were folded into a perfect square.

'Why has Papa left?' I asked, admittedly rather tactlessly.

'He hasn't left, Aurore. We've just decided to have a bit of time apart.'

'Are you getting divorced?'

The face my mother pulled in response suggested now was not the time to be asking these questions.

'When was it that you and Papa met again?'

'You know when. At the chapter of the Chevaliers.'

'Which one? When exactly?'

'You want the exact time and date?' she replied defensively.

'Yes.'

Bérengère put down the sheets.

'Why? What difference does it make?' she snapped.

Then she left the room, muttering that it wasn't easy to bring up a fifteen-year-old daughter.

That afternoon, I took advantage of my mother having to make a trip to Beaune to go through the family photo albums and pinpoint the date of the chapter of the Chevaliers du Tastevin. She had held on to the menu and programme for the evening at Vougeot.

If the doctor was right, then going back exactly nine months from my birth, my mother had not yet met François Delfer.

'Is François Delfer my father or not?' I asked abruptly at breakfast one morning before my brother had come down.

The slap came a fraction of a second later; just thinking about it, I can still feel the burn on my cheek.

'You little tart,' she shouted. 'How dare you ask that?'

I don't know if it was the slap or the words 'little tart' that shocked me the most. When I got back from school that evening, I didn't speak to her. After a meal lasting half an hour during which I hadn't said a word and only my brother had filled the silences by telling us about his school trip, Bérengère put down her cutlery before she had finished her dessert and muttered, 'This can't go on.' Still completely mute, I looked up at her as she stared at me in silence. That was when I knew the answer to my question. And I knew, too, that I was completely ready to hear it.

She asked my brother to give us a minute, then she got up, opened a drawer and took out a packet of Marlboros and a lighter. I chose not to remind her that she had given up smoking three years before. She put an ashtray down on the tablecloth, took out a cigarette and lit it. She took her first puff and closed her eyes.

'I didn't know I was pregnant, not straight away. Not when I came home ... Then I began to wonder; I was late, so I went to buy a test – not round here though; everyone knows everyone here. I got your Papy to drop me in Dijon; I told him I was meeting friends and asked if he would pick me up later that day. I bought the test in a chemist's and I couldn't concentrate on anything else all afternoon. I walked around town with the carrier bag from the chemist's tucked inside my handbag. I stopped for coffees at pavement cafés to pass the time. A month earlier, I was still in Paris at the École du Louvre; it seemed so recent and yet so far away. Everything had changed.'

'Was this when you used to sing?'

'Yes, that's right. It was when I was in a band ...'

She breathed out her smoke.

'My father came to collect me. I told him I'd had a great time. He was happy, seemed to have had his mind put at rest – it's crazy how easy it is to pull the wool over people's eyes. I got the result that evening: I was pregnant. I was terrified; I didn't know what I was going to say to my parents, which was ridiculous really – I was an adult, I could do what I liked ... The only person I would have liked to talk to about it wasn't there and I didn't know where he had gone. To the USA, but where? And impossible to reach, since there were no mobile phones in those days, no emails, nothing ... Yes, I could have called his brother, but what would I have said to him?'

She flicked her ash into the ashtray.

'Anyway, we had broken up, said goodbye, it was all over. What could I do, back in Burgundy? It was all ... too much.'

'You could have just had an abortion,' I said, immediately regretting it.

'That never crossed my mind,' she replied emphatically. 'Never,' she insisted, looking me straight in the eye.

I looked down.

'Then I met François. Two or three days later, I'm not sure exactly. My parents dragged me along to Vougeot. I didn't want to go, but they were so looking forward to it that I agreed. I had told them I had come round to the idea of taking on the running of the hotel and so they were keen to show off the daughter who would be taking over the family business. It was a big deal to them – they had been worried about me being an art student in Paris and even more so when I joined the band. They were afraid I'd become a junkie or something ... If I had done well at the École du Louvre, it would have been different ...'

She stubbed out her cigarette and immediately lit another.

'So I met your father, François, at Vougeot,' she continued. 'I had heard a lot about him; he was the son of one of Mamie's school friends and I knew they were all keen for us to meet. Such a cliché, now that I think about it ... That night at Vougeot, we drank a bit too much, went out into the vineyard and kissed. I'm not even sure why I did it, I just wanted to forget it all, start afresh, and I'll say it again, he was kind, thoughtful ... I wanted to forget ... everything. François and I went out on a date a few days after the kiss in the vineyard, then it became serious, very serious. He asked me to marry him, just like that, one evening; he seemed so sure ... I asked if I could think about it. I wanted to tell him I was pregnant with another man's baby but I couldn't do it; I thought it would ruin everything, our blossoming relationship, my parents, his parents. Then a thought occurred to me: maybe I didn't have to say anything at all ... There was only a three-week gap – men don't really understand these things,' she said with a smile. 'I only had to pretend the baby was early. François only came to the doctor with me once, a totally routine check-up. Every other time, I saw Dr Lessart on my own, and he didn't know the date I had met François. It was easy ... On top of that, François wasn't even there when you were born; he was on a wine trip to Singapore. Arriving three weeks premature, you'd still have been a bonnie baby; you wouldn't have needed to go in an incubator ... Lessart and I were the only ones who knew you weren't premature. Nobody blinked at the story. As soon as you arrived, all anybody was interested in was you and your smiles. The only person who might have guessed something was my mother,' she said softly, biting her bottom lip. 'I think she might have had her doubts, but we never spoke about it.'

'Who was he?' I asked. 'Who?' I said again when she failed to answer.

My mother stood up, walked back over to the cupboard with the cigarettes and opened one of the doors to take out a copy of *Challenges*, which the hotel subscribed to. Quite a few businessmen came to Burgundy with their families to recharge their batteries, and were glad to find this economics magazine on the coffee table with the others. She put it down in front of me. On the cover, a man with brown hair, a cat-like smile and eyes that, though slightly sad-looking, sparkled had his hands clasped in front of him and seemed to be paying a great deal of attention to whatever he was looking at. You could also see that his shirtsleeves were held together by elegant tiger's-eye cufflinks. The headline was 'JBM, birth of an emperor'.

'That's him,' my mother said matter-of-factly. 'Ask me whatever you like about him, but let me ask you something in return: however things are between me and François, I don't want you to tell him what you know and I don't want you telling your brother either. Promise me.'

I paused. Why would I go talking to François Delfer, and what could I possibly share with my eleven-year-old brother? Then I mumbled, 'I promise ...' without taking my eyes off the picture of JBM, and inside my head – I remember as if it was yesterday – I added in a whisper, '... to find him.'

675 x 564 = 380,700

From then on, Aurore's entire life became focused on one goal: to meet the man with the cat-like smile. Bérengère had told her how they met; about the band, Pierre, the antique broker, their trips to Le Relais de la Clef; and then how the relationship had ended. It was late by the time they said goodnight on the first-floor landing.

'I'm sorry,' Bérengère said, taking her daughter in her arms.

Aurore went into her room, closed the door behind her and fell onto her bed, burying her head under the pillow until she could barely breathe.

The magazine article described a secretive, charismatic and well-regarded businessman, and analysed his links with a powerful group she had never heard of, which ran a global chain of luxury hotels and casinos: Caténac. Jean-Bernard Mazart was married to Blanche de Caténac, a name that seemed like something out of a fairy tale. The man was light years away from François Delfer. The following year, François and Bérengère got divorced. Aurore kept her promise. She never told him that she knew he wasn't her father. He distanced himself from her and her mother and started a new life with another woman a few miles away.

There would be many steps to climb in order to reach JBM. Aurore set to work. She took herself from being an average student with little interest in school to a highly motivated pupil at the top of the class, and went on to study law and languages. If she was to work alongside JBM, she would need to master at least four languages; she learnt six. Her dedication to her studies gained her the affectionate nickname 'the Terminator' from her classmates. The years went by and JBM seemed as inaccessible as ever – the few times Aurore had sent her CV to the Arcadia group, she had only received stock replies to the effect that there were currently no openings. Aurore pursued her career as a PA, moving gradually up the ranks of responsibility, until, while working for the European Commission, she was told she would be attending a conference entitled 'Digital Europe, the last frontier'. Aurore was now an elegant young grey-suited woman of twenty-six.

She hardly slept for two nights before the conference. She went over and over her plan, like one of those criminals who spend weeks plotting a raid on a security van and a quick getaway, knowing the whole operation will be over in the space of five minutes. As for her, she would have mere seconds to play with. She spent the evenings practising in front of the mirror, acting out how she would approach him and shake his hand. 'Good evening, I'm Aurore Delfer and I'd very much like to work with you.' It was important to look him in the eye but without seeming too forceful or demanding. Arouse his curiosity. Everything depended on a few words. And then she did it; at the drinks reception after the conference, she had moved away from her colleagues at the Commission and waited for the men to stop talking to JBM. When he was finally alone for a few moments, she drained and put down her glass of champagne, took a deep breath and walked straight up to him, barging a man chewing a petit four out of her way. Once she was standing in front of JBM, she stopped, looked him in the eye and held out her hand, flashing him her best smile.

'Good evening, I'm Aurore Delfer and I'd very much like to work with you.'

The touch of his hand. Eleven years had passed since she had seen his face on the cover of *Challenges*, eleven years before she could touch him.

'Evening.' He smiled. 'And who might Aurore Delfer be?'

'One of Mario Moncelli's personal assistants.'

'Good,' JBM said softly, nodding his head, apparently impressed. 'And why do you want to work with me?'

Aurore started delivering the little spiel she had practised in front of the mirror, but he stopped her short.

'What's 675 times 564?' he asked with a smile.

Aurore closed her eyes and then opened them again to look straight at him.

'380,700.'

The smile vanished from JBM's face; he tilted his head and stared at Aurore, a serious look on his face. She felt as if everyone else in the huge room had disappeared, all the noise and conversations had ceased and only the two of them were left.

'Now that's not something I see every day. Let's try again,' he said in English.

'Try me,' Aurore challenged him, maintaining eye contact.

'8,765 minus 5,438?'

'... 3,327?'

'Aurore!' her manager called from across the room, indicating with a slight tilt of the head that it was about time she came back to join the group, even that talking to JBM in person was not entirely appropriate.

'I'd better go,' she excused herself, smiling apologetically.

'You're speaking to me,' JBM replied steadily, holding her gaze, 'so you can do what you want. Let me demonstrate.'

He waved amicably at the woman who had shouted at Aurore, accompanying the gesture with a perfectly false smile. The woman immediately raised her glass in their direction, all sweetness and light.

'There you go, sorted. Where were we ... How do you do it?'

'I can visualise numbers.'

'Me too.'

'Later,' JBM told a man who was on the verge of striking up a conversation but immediately turned on his heel.

'Now, you'd better give me your business card; that's what you came for, after all.'

'It is, but that's going to be tricky – Madame Crespin won't take her eyes off me,' she said, turning briefly towards the woman who had called her over.

'Where's your card?' JBM asked.

'In my jacket pocket.'

'OK. Take it out, hold it inside your hand using your thumb, and shake my hand. I'll take it from there.'

Aurore slipped her hand into her pocket and then held it out to shake with JBM; he took it in his grasp and she felt his fingers slide the business card under his shirt cuff. She took a few steps away before turning back to look at him. She had already been replaced by a circle of other delegates. They were talking to JBM, but he appeared disinterested. A minute later, she turned round again. He was gone.

Aurore was sorting out the change to pay for her coffee when she saw the door to the hotel swing open and JBM appear in the doorway. She stood up and the coins slid out of her hand, but she didn't hear them hit the ground. He crossed the road and walked towards her without taking his eyes off her, the emotion clear to see on his face. He came up the three steps to the café terrace and stopped in front of her. Aurore couldn't tear her gaze away from his as he stood looking at her as if for the first time. Then, without saying a word, he threw his arms tightly around her. Aurore would always remember how she had struggled to breathe; he couldn't seem to let go of her, as if the pair of them might be fixed in that position for eternity. And she would remember his breath on her neck, the suddenly shallow breathing that replaced all words.

Zénith and Semtex

'We're not going anywhere! We've been here for a thousand years!'

The Zénith arena was crammed with people that evening. Vaugan, without using notes, was pacing the stage with his clip-on microphone, haranguing the crowd. It had been forty minutes now since the extreme-right leader had started talking. His website, which was live-streaming his performance with English subtitles for his international audience, had had four hundred thousand views from across Europe. The day before, the *New York Times*, which was compiling a dossier on the extreme right in Europe, had run an article entitled 'Sébastien Vaugan – the man who won't be stopped'. The photograph showed the founder of France République (previously the WWP), chin raised in a pose worthy of Mussolini.

Vaugan had talked about the crime rate amongst 'immigrants born in France', the suburbs he himself came from (a son of the working class, a grandson of the working class, and working class myself!) and 'French people who were not really French and never would be'. He had then called for a moment's 'noise' to show condemnation of the 'black day' in 1976 when President Giscard d'Estaing and his prime minister Jacques Chirac had signed the family entry and resettlement law that allowed immigrant workers to bring their families over to France and base themselves and their descendants on French soil, where they had absolutely no business to be. And before getting onto the Islamisation of France ('I know that's the bit you're waiting for; you won't be disappointed') Vaugan had given his geopolitical views on the continent of Africa since the end of the post-war economic boom. Against the advice of his communications adviser, he had adopted an intimate tone with the audience and it seemed to be working.

'What is a revolution? It's when one caste replaces another, and the replacement is achieved with violence. Because all the legitimate, soft means have failed. That's what a revolution is. I know what you will say in response, friends; you will give the whining response of the sucker who has been brainwashed with ideas of humanism: "But Vaugan, you're mad, you've no idea; these Africans don't have the means to revolt. They are poor and sad. They're sunk in poverty, and that's why they want to come here." Really? Are you joking? Haven't you noticed that when the Africans took up their machetes and decided to go to war with the next-door village, there was blood spilt everywhere. Has it escaped you that those Africans were not exactly intellectual humanists! They're the best in the world at two things: the machete and running ...'

When Vaugan finished with Usain Bolt's famous victory gesture, there was thunderous applause.

'Why don't they revolt against their pseudo-dictators? Why do they come and create disorder here instead of creating order back home? Why is that then? What are they waiting for to overthrow their Negro bosses grown rich on so-called global capitalism?'

The communications adviser raised an eyebrow. It was 'black' that had been in the script, not 'Negro'.

'Why don't they seize power, roll up their sleeves and get building, building, goddamn it! Cities, roads, bridges, as all countries have had to do at some point in their history. Here, in our beautiful country, there was a time when there was nothing but little villages with terrible roads that led nowhere and forests full of wolves! Is it still like that today, I ask you? No! Why? Because one day we decided to do something about it and we built cities, roads, bridges and ports; we created craftsmen; we used iron and coal; we put mills in the water to mill wheat. They can't even be bothered to dig wells, although we tried to teach them sixty years ago!'

More thunderous applause and catcalls.

'We made things grow and we sold them; we developed our trade. Why are these goddamn countries not capable of doing the same? Why are they lagging behind the rest of humanity? ... Because they are like lazy sloths. Sloths asleep in the sun without a care in the world!'

Another round of rhythmic applause in the arena.

'Shall I tell you the solution? The solution we've been looking for now for fifty years? I'll tell you ...'

Vaugan paused proudly, before bellowing, 'We'll re-colonise them! Since you're no good at anything, we'll come and show you! Good news, eh? Don't move, we're on our way! We have to come back and make an inventory. We left them with flourishing countries, and we'll be going back to rubble, but never mind, we'll take it on; France is magnanimous!'

The arena was in raptures, and laughing. Vaugan mopped his brow, laughing too, before assuming a sober expression.

'And all these immigrants who are landing on us like swarms of locusts, who I hear referred to as poor unfortunates who have paid a lot of money for their journey and have been exploited by smugglers … What do we care?!' yelled Vaugan. 'Do you analyse the psychology of the locust who lands on your field to munch up your harvest? Do you consult books of entomology to find out who your locust is: locust, who are you; where do you come from? Of course you don't! You don't give a shit what the damned insect is, you just want to protect your field, your labour, your work. And you want to keep the pests out!'

'Out! Out! Out!' came the chants.

'Have you seen the images coming from Italy? From Lampedusa? From Calais? Because you find these people in Calais – they're attacking the poor lorry drivers so that they can get to England. Apparently there are Ethiopians and Eritreans – I don't know where Eritrea is, and I don't want to know. Do you think they look like poor people? … They look like what they are: thugs! Barbarians!' shouted Vaugan, over the wild clapping. 'Barbarians,' he went on, 'come to crowbar open the frontiers of Europe. They are thieves! As for the boats in the Mediterranean that people cry over because they're stuffed with five hundred migrants, when they can only fit ninety … The coastguards shouldn't go and save them; on the contrary!' Vaugan was working himself up. 'They should make waves! Waves and even more waves!'

Delight in the crowd.

'Let's go to all the coasts!' cried Vaugan, walking over to the edge of the stage. 'Let's put our hands in the water' – here he gestured with his hands – 'and make waves!' He waved his hands frenetically.

'Waves! Waves! Waves! Waves!' they chanted like a war cry.

'Illegal immigrants … Oh, the illegal immigrants' – now he puffed his chest out – 'beloved by hipsters and champagne socialists, beloved by elites and celebrities! Their pastime, their hobby!' spluttered Vaugan. '"But what are we going to do with all these illegal immigrants? What are we going to do with these poor people? What can we do for them?"' Vaugan mimicked a concerned face that was not unlike Jack Nicholson in *The Shining*. 'Since they have no papers, they can bugger off! Simple! Do you think that if I go to the US and disappear into the crowd and start working illegally for ten or fifteen years, I can just show up one morning at a demo in the streets of Washington or New York? Do you think I can do that? That I'd be able to shout slogans in the street with a placard complaining that America hasn't given me an American passport even though I work illegally on her soil. D'you think that would work?' yelled Vaugan. 'Would there be Yanks willing to form humanitarian aid groups for arseholes like me? No! They would boot me out back here!'

The crowd loved it. From all sides they shouted, 'Vaugan, Vaugan!'

Vaugan stood centre stage in the spotlight.

'France République defines the right wing of the right: "To the Right of the Right", that's our slogan. Are you frightened of being to the right of the right? Hey, Russian comrade, tovarish! Come and talk to me,' shouted Vaugan, cupping his hands round his mouth. 'Hey, Mr American President, get your arse out of the Oval Office and come and talk to me! Chancellor Merkel, put on your little jacket and come and talk to me! Her British Majesty's Prime Minister, come and talk to me! Leave the riches of the Élysée, President of France, and come and talk to me! Hey! People of France! People of France, come and talk to me!'

Vaugan threw his arms wide open. The crowd was ecstatic and a good quarter of the Zénith was on its feet.

'Workers, farmers, middle managers and senior executives, middle classes, the unemployed, retirees who have money, graduates with no work, I'm calling on everyone who has been let down ...'

His communications adviser began to scrabble feverishly through the speech – none of that had been anywhere in the text.

'... I'm calling on all the people without qualifications, without hope, without money; I'm calling on all the people all over the country; I'm calling on the men of the past: rise from your tombs, remember your past glories, take up your arms again, your eagles, your crowns; I call on Napoleon, Clovis, Charlemagne, St Louis; I call on the blood of our fallen on the battlefields of honour; I call on France ... to rise up!' He raised his arms and threw his head back.

Now half of the Zénith crowd was standing, fists raised, chanting Vaugan's name. Others applauded, their arms above their heads. Some were drumming their feet, and flags waved frenetically. Vaugan could see in the pit some young people who hadn't really understood the change in the right's message and were giving fascist salutes. But overall the mood was pleasant, with all those arms outstretched towards him. 'Down with Europe! Down with Brussels!' yelled some overexcited men. As the clamour grew, Vaugan prepared to deliver the second part of his speech.

'Now?' asked the man in grey.

'Just wait one moment,' replied the voice in his earpiece.

'Now, I'm going to talk to you about people who are suffering and about whom no one ever speaks, far off in our beautiful

173

provinces … and I'm going to talk about the mosques that are sprouting like mushrooms in those same provinces and which are subsidised to the tune of millions of euros of your money, and I'm going to talk about the last remaining parish priests who live off one boiled egg a day and who perform mass in front of church pews that are three-quarters empty. I'm going to talk to you about the collapse of our country!' bellowed Vaugan.

'Now!' said the voice.

The man in grey, who had been holding a digital device the size of a mobile phone in his pocket since the beginning of the meeting, pressed the button and closed his eyes. There was a blinding light with Vaugan's platform at the epicentre. The three Semtex charges, each twenty kilos, exploded exactly as planned and the platform tipped backwards, dragging Vaugan down with it. The noise was brief but deafening, then smoke began to rise. The platform had gone, the front rows were no longer cheering, but for the most part, the blood on their faces and hands was due to their eardrums bursting.

'All done,' declared the man in grey, soberly, before moving away through the crowd to the exit.

A Three-legged Dog

The next morning, Aurore had opened the shutters to discover the vines were shrouded in dense fog. She found her mother watching the news of the bombing of the Zénith. Vaugan was reported to be in a coma and eleven others were seriously wounded, including, most severely, his publicist. The investigation was under way and the journalists were already deep in speculation: a split between factions of the far right? Islamic extremists? The explosives used in the attack suggested 'well-trained, if not professional elements'.

'He's already had his breakfast,' said Bérengère, 'and gone out with a bag, heading towards Romanée-Conti. I shouldn't have let him go on his own, he'll get lost.' She frowned at the fog outside the windows.

'I'll go,' said Aurore.

She picked out a parka and walked to the door.

The night before, JBM had put his arms around Bérengère, hugged her and whispered, 'Thank you.'

'What for?' Bérengère asked quietly but, rather than answer her, JBM continued, 'I'm sorry. I'm sorry for everything ...'

Then he felt very weary.

'Do you have to go back to Paris?' Bérengère asked. 'Why don't you stay, if you like? There are rooms free.'

JBM glanced at Aurore. They were both thinking of the

same person: Blanche. The Paris–New York flight took seven hours, so she would not yet have landed and probably wouldn't try to contact him until tomorrow. She would therefore be none the wiser about JBM's trip to Burgundy.

'We'll stay,' JBM decided.

The fog now covered all the vines. What he was looking for – the stone cross marking the entrance to the Romanée-Conti estate – was, according to Bérengère, 'at the end of Rue du Temps Perdu, but you don't have to take that road; you can cut across the vineyards.'

'I don't need to go *in search of lost time*?' JBM had asked with a smile. 'Sure about that?'

He stopped and looked around. He couldn't see five metres ahead of him.

'Everything is an amalgam of elements,' whispered JBM, remembering the phrase Pierre used to like to quote. 'I'm in the eye of the storm; there is no sky; everything is an amalgam of elements; there's nothing but mountains of water around me' – the last radio message sent from the *Manureva* by Alain Colas at four in the morning on 16 November 1978 off the coast of the Azores. That winter, both brothers had been glued to the incredible Route du Rhum transatlantic solo race and the news of the sailor's tragic disappearance; the search for the boat and its skipper went on for several weeks, but no trace of either was ever found. At the time, Pierre became fixated on one particular detail, which, to his mind, was what the whole story turned on: Alain Colas didn't have his distress beacon with him. The signals the device emitted on an international frequency might have been picked up by aircraft or shipping vessels up to seventy-two hours after the distress call. He had simply forgotten to take it with him when he set off – it had been found in a bag on Quai Vauban in Saint-Malo.

JBM was working out which way to go – carry straight on or veer right through the vines? – when a little shadow emerged from the fog, a small dog running towards him whose front right leg was missing. JBM put down his bag, crouched down and held out his hand, which the little dog licked frantically while managing to balance very well on its three spindly legs. JBM stroked it between the ears.

'What happened to you, then, you poor old thing?'

The dog barked excitedly several times, as happy little dogs do.

'I'm lost,' JBM told him. 'I was trying to get to Romanée-Conti ... Do you want to take me back home?'

The creature barked again and began to head into the fog, following the path that ran alongside the vines. JBM went after him as he bounded down the track. They walked together for a good minute and then the dog stopped, sat himself down and, tongue lolling, looked up at JBM. There was a shift in the air and a few metres ahead of them, JBM made out the mighty Christian cross, built of stone six centuries earlier, which marked the entrance to the legendary Romanée-Conti estate.

'Thank you, my friend,' whispered JBM, patting the dog's back.

A stone cross, a wine estate and the valley it sat in – nothing about this mist-covered landscape had changed since the time of Charles VII.

'You found Jimmy then ...'

JBM turned round to see Aurore coming through the fog.

'He belongs to the estate, so he's just the guy to show you the way here.'

She bent down towards Jimmy, who began wagging his tail.

'With you to meet me here,' added JBM.

'Yes.' Aurore smiled. 'I'm your three-legged dog.'

'No, you're my beloved daughter.'

They looked at one another without speaking, and then Aurore's gaze settled on the bag.

'He said he wanted "a place of beauty and history". This is it, isn't it?'

'This is it.'

JBM reached down, unzipped the bag, carefully took out the urn and removed the lid. Aurore took a step backwards and stood very straight. The dog sat and watched intently.

'Let's go further into the vines,' suggested JBM. 'Pierre will be more in his element.'

They took three steps; the dog followed them and settled back down at their feet. The wind changed, blowing towards the vines, and beginning to break up the fog. Aurore crossed herself. JBM tipped the urn forward and, caught in a ray of sunlight, the ashes began to pour out, rising up around the cross before being carried off on the wind above the vines. When the urn was almost empty, JBM tapped the bottom to release the last few particles of the antiquarian. He placed it at the foot of the cross and stepped back again. The fog had almost blown away. JBM, Aurore and the dog remained silent for a long while, their gazes and thoughts lost in their surroundings. The dog barked once.

'Ceremony over,' remarked JBM.

Rats

Karim the Tuileries' park-keeper was deep in his reading of *L'Équipe* but glanced up at *Bubble*. Several women had just screamed and he had immediately thought it might be a flasher. They had already had one individual in a raincoat showing off his bits to passers-by. Karim had chased him down a path and wrestled the terrified man to the ground. The bloke had begged him not to call the police and even offered him money if he would let him go.

But this time Karim hadn't seen anyone acting suspiciously. The problem seemed to be on the ground, in the dust. Karim got up from his chair, dropping his paper.

'Stay back,' he called in French and then in English. He blew his whistle.

But the walkers, whether they were French or foreign, needed no second bidding and had already fled. Karim spoke into his walkie-talkie. 'Karim, at the entrance. I've got a problem, a huge problem.'

'What's going on, Karim?' came the crackly response.

'Rats! I don't know where they've appeared from but there are dozens of them. They're all making for the structure.'

'Don't be ridiculous!'

'I'm not being ridiculous – come and see for yourself! They're coming from every direction.'

Now there had to be hundreds of the rodents, ranged in what looked like battle formation round the pond. A brave tourist walked towards them to take a picture on his phone. The rats froze at his approach.

'Be careful! Stay away from them!'

It was the first time that Karim had seen the rats behaving in an obviously aggressive manner. One of them jumped on the tourist's ankle and climbed in a scrabbling of legs up to the man's face. The man's wife screamed as the man waved his arms frantically until the rat fell to the ground and went to join the others.

'Are you all right?' Karim asked the man who had gone over to his wife and children and was touching his face with his hands.

'*Sì! Sto bene, ma cos'è successo qui?*' cried the tourist, looking furious.

Karim didn't know how to reply and looked over at the horde of rats. It really was like a commando operation. Arranged in a circle around the pond, some rats were standing guard, while others in groups of two or three were frantically nibbling the cables that secured *Bubble*. Each cable had a group of rats, and as soon as Karim tried to approach, the guard rats immediately adopted an attack pose.

'Karim!' shouted a voice.

Five park-keepers, one of whom was his boss carrying a loudhailer, were jogging towards him. They all stopped to catch their breath and look at the spectacle.

'What the hell?' said the head park-keeper in alarm.

'They're eating the cables,' Karim told him tonelessly. 'All the cables,' he added.

Just then one of the cables broke free with a loud snap, immediately followed by a second one. One of the rats was catapulted into the air.

'But ... but ...' stammered the boss, 'they're going to release that monstrosity – and have you seen the size of it? And the wind's getting up ...Franck,' he said, turning towards one of the park-keepers, 'call the fire brigade immediately!'

In twenty-five years of guarding the park, the head park-keeper had never had to think as fast on his feet. 'We'll evacuate the gardens to the east, as quickly as possible,' he announced just as a third cable popped into the air with a sound like the crack of a whip. He took his loudhailer and spoke into the microphone. 'Evacuation of the Tuileries Gardens. Everyone is to leave the gardens.

'Please leave the gardens by the east exit, the exit by the Louvre!'

Then he activated the siren on the loudhailer. Three cables snapped almost simultaneously and *Bubble* began to rock. The tourists assembled at the east end of the pond but, fascinated by what was happening, did not seem in a hurry to leave the park.

'Where's the bloody fire brigade, for God's sake!' complained the head keeper, as two more cables gave way, projecting a rat into the air which then landed at his feet, causing him to jump.

The rat righted itself and scurried off to join the others.

'How much does the installation weigh?' he asked nervously.

'I don't know,' replied Karim.

The last cables snapped and *Bubble* broke free. A great shout went up across the park as the structure began to lift off the ground.

*

No clear explanation for what had happened was ever given. The most likely cause was advanced a few weeks later. Since *Bubble* covered the pond, which was the main water source for the park rats, they had decided to get rid of the impediment that was preventing them from quenching their thirst. Rat specialists saw the incident as a brilliant demonstration of the abilities of their favoured species.

Now floating ten metres above the ground, *Bubble* moved with grace. Tourists had taken out their phones and, in order to capture the work for ever on their memory cards, extended their arms towards the work as if performing some ancestral rite of allegiance. The rats, rapid and furtive, had departed for their hiding places as fast as they had appeared. A strange silence now reigned over the gardens, and the wind created little ripples on the rubberised canvas of the giant brain which seemed to make it even more like a living being. *Bubble* drifted gently over towards the gardens' gates, heading towards Place de la Concorde. The tourists, gazing upwards, walked in silence, as though following a mysterious deity. Some, their arm still outstretched, must be filming a video on their phones, giving them the wild-eyed look and strange gait of sleepwalkers.

Bubble rose higher as it entered Place de la Concorde. Now it was exactly twenty-five metres above the ground, just over the Obelisk. Cars stopped suddenly and screeching tyres, crunching bodywork and swearing could be heard. In the distance a scooter driver righted his bike and limped off. One after the other, vehicles stopped and drivers got out, shading their eyes to look upwards.

Soon Place de la Concorde was blocked and there was a growing clamour of horns coming from cars on the Champs-Élysées which stopped when drivers there also got out and stared in amazement or whipped out their phones. *Bubble* seemed to create a collective reflex in onlookers, causing them to look up and extend their arms towards it.

The structure seemed to be hesitating between warm and cold currents of air when a siren blared briefly, announcing the arrival of a fire engine in front of the park gates. Several men in uniform got out and went over to the park-keepers without taking their eyes off the giant brain floating above Place de la Concorde.

The chief fire officer asked what on earth was hovering above the Obelisk.

'It's *Bubble*,' replied Karim. 'It was over the pond; now it's up there ...'

'I see. And how did it get there?'

'The park rats released it ...'

The man nodded and said, 'Rats, well, you can explain that one later. But for now ... why is it floating?'

'I think it's filled with helium.'

'This just gets better,' said the fire officer. 'How big is it?'

'The same size as the pond, sixty metres.'

'OK. We'll have to call Aviation Safety.'

Bubble was now more than forty metres above the ground. Karim turned back towards the park. In front of the gates, journalists and cameramen, microphones in hand, were interviewing witnesses. Other press cars and motorbikes continued to arrive. The tourists and other pedestrians who had filmed or photographed the events were already uploading their images to social media and the continuous news networks had interrupted their programming to stream what was happening at Place de la Concorde.

*

Stan Lepelle was working in his studio in Yvelines on his latest project, a football in the form of a polyhedron. He decided to take a break, switched on the television and went to pour himself some carrot juice. When he returned, he found he was looking at his own face – his official photo with the frowning look of the artist preoccupied with the major issues of his day. Then that image disappeared to be replaced by a picture of *Bubble* in the skies of Paris, escorted by a helicopter on the way to the Eiffel Tower. The glass of carrot juice slid from Lepelle's hand and smashed on the tiles.

The Glory of *Bubble*

Helicopter EC145 from Civil Security followed *Bubble* for twenty minutes before concluding that any attempt to harpoon the structure would be impossible without endangering the aircraft and its crew. They had brought back astonishing pictures of the brain gliding over the city, which had been shown on television and shared across the web. Foreign TV stations had immediately picked up the bizarre images. From CNN to NHK, news channels showed the surreal pictures of the giant brain floating above the French capital on loop. The feared collision with the Eiffel Tower had been avoided, *Bubble* having expertly risen in a series of jolts as if trying to escape its tormentor – or taunt it. When *Bubble* reached six hundred metres above the ground, the helicopter was relieved of its mission and the authorities took a very French decision: they would do nothing.

Until *Bubble* had risen above the height flown by short- and long-haul flights, pilots had no other option than to circle over Paris waiting for the brain to decide to fly off upwards. *Bubble* was still gaining height and speed. Even though it was not at all the aerodynamic shape of hot-air balloons, Michel Chevalet (known and loved by the French for his explanations of scientific matters over the last forty years on various TV channels) said on i-Télé that *Bubble* had 'mutated into a kind of weather balloon' very similar to the one launched from Japan in September

2013 which had also measured sixty metres in diameter. That balloon held the record for the highest unmanned flight of an inflatable structure and had reached the mesosphere, that is to say, it had reached 53.7 kilometres in height. Other scientists disagreed with Michel Chevalet, pointing out that the Japanese balloon had been made of an exceptional material, only 0.003 millimetres thick, which was not the case with *Bubble*. 'That's true,' conceded Chevalet, but he went on excitedly, '*Bubble*, though, has been constructed from a rubberised material, BN657, never before tested in the atmosphere. It's a sort of genetically modified rubber, if you'll excuse the simplification, and so no one knows how it will react. It's rising more slowly, but it's possible that it will rise as high, or even higher!' Michel Chevalet had then launched into a description of the secondary effects of the thermosphere, and the ionosphere if it rose that high, which would cause *Bubble* to expand into a perfect sphere before its inevitable implosion.

Stan Lepelle was fascinated. On Google his name was now associated with two million results and images of his works had all been replaced by pictures of the giant airborne brain. The recognition and celebrity he had craved for so long had finally arrived. His art dealer had called, over the moon. Without even saying who was calling, he had reeled off ecstatically, 'It's amazing. It's extraordinary. It's like a prophecy. Emails are flooding in from all over the world. The phone hasn't stopped ringing. Everyone wants you! I'm going to ask the Qataris to double their offer. It's rising, rising! It's rising as fast as your stock, Stan, it's magic!'

'It is indeed a prophecy,' replied Lepelle, seriously.

'TV reporters are asking to interview you. I've given them your address – they're going to come and do it live. Make sure you look after them well. I'll ring you back, I have another call coming in.'

The dealer hung up before Lepelle had the chance to point out that he should have asked before giving out his home address to journalists. But none of it mattered any more. He felt a preternatural calm, a strange, saintly feeling of well-being somewhere between languor and floating. Ivana had disappeared after he had destroyed the giant stud and some of his pots of acrylic paint with a poker. She had not been in her room when he had gone up to see. He had not bothered to try to track her down on her mobile. It was obvious that she had upped and left. Already the memory of the beautiful Russian seemed distant.

After the phone call, Lepelle went into the corridor leading to the record room. From the living room he could hear the news getting back to French and international politics. But the end of the news programme would again turn to *Bubble*, now even higher above the earth – a happy story offering a little bit of magic to a world on the edge of the abyss, a little bit of magic he had provided. He, Stan Lepelle, 'the famous French contemporary artist' as he was now known.

He pushed the door open. The sun flooded the parquet floor and shelves. Lepelle moved softly round the room, his fingers gliding over the slate fittings, and went over to his drum kit. He touched the cold golden metal of the cymbals, gave them a flick that set them spinning, then turned to the shelves that held the songs and albums he had helped create. In another life. The phrase 'another life' seemed to appear to him with a clarity he had never experienced before. It was as if he were seeing the words floating in the room and gently bouncing off the walls. Two words: 'another' and 'life'. His drumsticks lay on the drum stool and he picked them up and looked at them before clamping them together and breaking them over his knee with a sharp snap. He put the pieces on the floor by the drums and went out, turning the key in the lock. He padded silently over to the window of the American-style kitchen. He opened the window wide, feeling the fresh air on his face, closed his eyes and threw the key as far as he could into the garden. He didn't even hear it land. It must have ended up somewhere in the grass or in a flower bed. He wouldn't be able to find it again. The rain would ensure it was buried in the earth and it would rust underground until it disintegrated. The room with the records would stay closed for ever.

His thoughts were interrupted by the bell at the front gates. He went to the bay window in the living room and saw cars and motorbikes parked with at least twenty cameramen and journalists. A lorry bearing a satellite dish was manoeuvring in the street. He pressed the intercom button. 'Come in,' he said, pressing another button to open the gates.

As the day wore on, journalists from TV stations all over the world arrived at Lepelle's house. The reporters were ordered not to leave the artist. As long as *Bubble* continued to break altitude records, they were to stay close to its creator and wait for his comment. The new arrivals put their equipment in the living room and busied themselves with their connections and video playbacks, when they were not helping themselves to fruit juice in the kitchen. Practically every language was being spoken in the living room and the ground floor resembled a film set organised entirely around one man: Stan Lepelle. The Japanese, who were the least obtrusive, addressed him with great respect, while the CNN reporters clapped him on the shoulder as if he'd won a great sporting event.

When *Bubble* had broken the record set by Felix Baumgartner (the parachutist who had ejected from his astronaut's capsule thirty-nine kilometres above the ground) the company that manufactured BN657 rubber (*made in France* as the news services were keen to point out) began to tweet about the unexpected resilience of their product, and also about their stock price which had just risen 32 per cent. At fifty-four kilometres above earth *Bubble* broke the record set by Japan for an unmanned balloon flight, and the Japanese reporters from NHK looked at Lepelle with even more respect. Michel Chevalet was jubilant when the structure reached eighty kilometres; now it had broken into the ionosphere. According to Chevalet, it was possible that *Bubble* would reach the Kármán Line.

'What is the Kármán Line, Michel?' the journalist asked Chevalet.

'The Kármán Line lies at an altitude of 328,084 feet above the earth's surface, that's to say 100 kilometres, at the level where atmospheric pressure disappears. Or to put it more simply, it's the frontier between us and outer space. If it crosses that line, *Bubble* will have entered outer space.'

Lepelle had just finished an interview with Korean TV when the phone rang.

'He's buying it!' shouted his dealer. 'François Pinault has just bought *Bubble*.'

Lepelle sat down on one of the few unoccupied chairs in the living room. 'The press release from Agence France-Presse has just arrived,' continued the dealer. 'I'll read it to you: "François Pinault, the billionaire and contemporary art collector, has just announced his intention to buy the ephemeral structure *Bubble* for an undisclosed sum.'" Then he crowed, 'Do you want me to tell you how much he's paying?'

'Later,' replied Lepelle.

And he hung up.

When *Bubble* did pass the Kármán Line, the company manu-facturing BN657 announced its stock had risen 620 per cent since the beginning of the day. The synthetic rubber *Bubble* was made of could be put to infinite uses, both civil and military. Now the images reaching television stations were coming from the International Space Station, ISS, whose telescope showed *Bubble* floating over the rounded shape of the earth.

'This is the most beautiful day of my career,' breathed the dealer, who had come to join Lepelle in Yvelines. 'We'll take the ISS photos and make limited-edition copies in partnership with the Pinault Foundation. You can sign them ... It's going to be wonderful.' He was almost sobbing as he hugged the artist.

Lepelle had made art history. He was more famous than Warhol, more famous than Jeff Koons. He actually felt, for a brief euphoric moment, as though he had become as well known as Leonardo da Vinci.

Rue de Moscou

'If he pulls it off, which is not in doubt, it will be a first for astronomy, a first for art and a first for science all at the same time. Stan Lepelle is with us. Welcome, Stan ...'

'Hello,' replied Lepelle, smiling.

'You're talking to us from your studio in Yvelines ...'

Lepelle no longer wore the frown of the concerned intellectual. Now his smile seemed youthful, making him appear as likeable as in the days of the Holograms.

'You have brought glory to France!' began the journalist who must have been trained in reporting on competitive sport rather than art and culture. 'I think we have the new images from the ISS,' he went on as a video of rare beauty played behind him, showing the brain floating above the planet.

'But we at BFM-TV also have a surprise for you, Stan Lepelle: we have a direct line to the cosmonauts of the ISS,' the journalist announced proudly. 'ISS, are you receiving?' he said, pressing his earpiece into his ear. 'Can you hear us? This is French television ...'

Alain muted the sound. He had returned home after a day of visiting patients. Many of the apartments he had visited had a television in the patient's bedroom. So he along with his patients had been able to follow *Bubble*'s adventure all the way into outer space. Alain was one of the few doctors still to do home visits – almost no general practitioners still offered them. In fact, fewer people now wanted to become doctors, least of all GPs. *Le Quotidien du médecin* had recently published an edifying article on the 'French medical desert': older doctors were retiring and there was no one to replace them. The article cited the example of a Romanian woman doctor whose arrival was eagerly awaited by the residents of one of the cantons of Lozère. But that in turn caused a problem, since Romania was also lacking in doctors and having to recruit GPs from Ukraine or Lithuania.

The apartment was silent. Véronique had left that morning for an interior design fair at Porte de Versailles and had let him know that she would not be home until dinner time. After making himself coffee, Alain turned to the day's mail that Madame Da Silva had posted through the door. There were the usual invoices and flyers, but also a handwritten envelope addressed to him. He was about to open it, when the doorbell rang. Alain got up and called through the door to ask who was there.

'Ivana,' replied the voice.

'Ivana …' murmured Alain as he opened the door.

'I don't know if you remember me?' she said, standing in the doorway, a suitcase on wheels at her side.

'Yes, I do remember … it would be hard to forget you,' he replied, noticing that the young woman he had only ever seen lying down was a good head taller than him.

'I have something for you. Can I come in?'

'Yes, of course,' said Alain, standing aside to let her pass. 'In here,' he said, indicating the waiting room which served as the living room when there were no patients.

Ivana went in, dragging her suitcase.

'Are you going somewhere?'

'Yes, I'm going back to Russia; my flight is in a couple of hours. After that I might go to California – I have friends there. Oh, so you're watching this too?' she asked, pointing to the television, which showed pictures of *Bubble* in outer space. 'It's good. He must be happy; everyone's talking about him, and that's what he wanted.'

'Don't you live with him any more?'

'No, I left him,' she said, taking off her leather jacket.

'I'm sorry,' said Alain, automatically.

'No need!' exclaimed Ivana, sitting herself confidently down on the sofa. 'It's better this way. Much better. More straightforward.' There was a short silence then Ivana asked if he had any whisky.

Alain nodded.

'Pour me a whisky. Lepelle doesn't drink; there is only vegetable juice at his house – organic carrot, artichoke, algae. I'm sick of it.'

'Ice? Water?' offered Alain from the dining room.

'No ice or water! Just as it comes,' replied Ivana.

Alain came back into the living room with a bottle of Bowmore and two glasses. He drew his armchair closer to the sofa.

'Stop,' she said, when he had poured the right amount.

The amount seemed very precise and he served himself the same.

'Chin chin …' said Alain, a little disconcerted by the Russian's presence in his sitting room.

They clinked glasses and each drank a mouthful.

'Are you all on your own here?'

'Yes, it's my day for home visits so I don't need my receptionist today.'

'Don't you have a wife either?'

'Yes,' replied Alain, smiling, 'I do have a wife. She's at an exhibition for work at Porte de Versailles. At least I think she is ...' He swirled his whisky in its glass.

'You think or you know?'

Alain smiled grimly, then looked Ivana in the eye. 'My wife is cheating on me. So I never really know where she is ...'

Alain was surprised to find himself being so open, reflecting that sometimes it is easier to tell the most intimate things about your life to complete strangers you will never see again – precisely because they are strangers you will never see again.

'That's not good,' said Ivana, in a disapproving tone that surprised him. Perhaps it was a remnant of Soviet rigidity.

'No, it's not good,' Alain agreed. He took another mouthful of whisky. 'Not long ago, I asked her if she was cheating on me. I was hoping she would say no, and she did. But I knew she was lying, so I was quite annoyed with her for not saying yes. It's complicated between couples ... I should leave her, but I can't make myself – we've been together for such a long time.'

'Shh,' said Ivana, placing a finger on Alain's lips. 'Your wife isn't here, and I won't be here long.'

Her long fingers glided over Alain's cheek and through his hair.

'What are you doing?' he whispered.

'I came to bring you your songs,' she said softly, 'the tracks made by your group. Lepelle kept everything. I put them all on a USB stick for you.'

'The songs ...' murmured Alain, and he wasn't sure if his feeling of giddiness came from the reappearance of the songs or from Ivana's hand which was now stroking his neck and proceeding towards the top button of his shirt.

'Who are you? A model or something like that?'

'Shh, you're talking too much. No more talking,' she said, getting nearer so that she could more easily undo the second button and then the third button of his shirt. 'Some people say that life is short,' she murmured in his ear, 'but my grandfather says that life is long and boring ... You understand? Do you understand?' she repeated, looking at him seriously.

Alain wasn't sure he understood any longer, but Ivana's hands, which had finished unbuttoning his shirt, seemed to be saying that if life were as long and boring as a grey sky, it was important to seize the moments of sun when they appeared. Ivana took off her boots and socks then stood up and stripped off her skirt and denim shirt. Alain was still looking at her when she deftly reached behind her back and unhooked her bra. Standing in front of him, she gazed at him in silence and Alain held his hand out to her perfect body, as if to check that it was real, that Ivana actually was standing in his waiting room, wearing only little white knickers, and that she was not a product of his imagination. Her skin felt incredibly smooth, as did her rounded breasts and especially her gorgeous flat stomach. She lay down on the sofa and put her bare feet on the arm. Alain wondered how many people had sat on this sofa. Millions perhaps. He had had it re-covered but it dated back to his father's time.

'Come here,' she said, and he joined her with the caution required of a man approaching a splendid, wild feline.

Their first kiss was gentle; the ones following, at Ivana's instigation, were more insistent, more avid, and for a brief moment, it was as if he were kissing Bérengère at Gare de Lyon. Better even – as if Ivana comprised all the Bérengères of all lost youth. The years dropped away, the past floated off, only the present counted, and there was no future. Nothing existed except their two bodies encountering each other on the sofa, then the same bodies getting up and going to the bedroom to lie down on the bed without a word and resume their frantic kissing and their caresses that became more and more targeted. Nothing existed except this girl who was offering herself to him and demanding nothing in return. Nothing mattered except the fact of being alive, astonishingly alive, somewhere in Western Europe at the beginning of the twenty-first century.

As Ivana's body quivered in the semi-darkness of the bedroom, and she let out gentle moaning sounds that rose to the ceiling, high above the clouds, the birds and the aeroplanes, in the infinity of space, under the cosmic pressure that had inflated it into an almost perfect sphere, *Bubble* imploded in the silence of the Galaxy. The debris disintegrated as it fell back to earth, making a fleeting mark across the sky like a shooting star.

A Letter (2)

Ivana had left. She may have been the one taking the flight to Russia, but it was Alain who seemed to be suffering the effects of jet lag. As if his internal clock had come too close to a source of radiation that had confused his synapses.

'Take me to Russia with you,' he clearly remembered saying to Ivana as he held her close. The apartment was very still; only a single ray of light filtered through the bedroom curtains. He had never uttered anything quite so insane, yet he had never been more deadly serious.

'You're mad,' Ivana had gently replied.

'I could cure people … That's what I do. Is there a doctor in your village?' Alain had asked hopefully.

'You're mad,' Ivana had repeated.

In the waiting room, Alain finished his whisky, then he finished Ivana's too. He stood up, took the bottle and put it back in the drinks cabinet, rinsed the glasses in the kitchen sink, dried them, and replaced them in the cupboard too. In the bedroom he opened the window wide, then removed the pillowcases and the sheets, piling them in the centre of the room. Then he crawled over the bed inspecting the mattress cover and headboard, looking for an incriminating long brown hair – but he found none. He returned to the kitchen, put the sheets and pillowcases in the washing machine and set them to wash on what he thought was a suitable programme. Véronique would probably be surprised he had washed the sheets, but would not pursue it. It would never occur to her that a young girl born in Siberia twenty-five years earlier would have undressed in the living room then led Alain to the bedroom to make love with him, before taking a plane to Moscow. Before Véronique got home, perhaps Alain would be able to come up with one of those explanations that make up the charm of domestic life: a cup of coffee carelessly spilt on the bed as he passed, a dirty mark left by his medical bag ... In the bathroom cupboard Alain found clean sheets and two new pillowcases. He remade the bed and contemplated the result.

Nothing remained of Ivana's visit. All traces, right down to her DNA, had been erased. Alain closed the bedroom door and went to take a shower. Then he dressed in clean clothes and sat down in his waiting room. As he listened to the distant churning of the washing machine's first cycle, his eye fell on the day's post which was still waiting on the low table. He had been about to open it when Ivana rang the bell. It seemed as if an entire week had passed since then. Alain tore open the handwritten envelope and began to read.

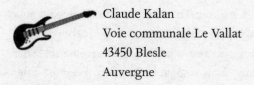

Claude Kalan
Voie communale Le Vallat
43450 Blesle
Auvergne

Dear Dr Massoulier

I received your recent letter along with the photocopy of the earlier letter sent by my previous employer, Polydor.

I appreciate you writing to me and I can understand how surprised you must have been to receive that encouraging reply from Polydor thirty-three years after sending them your demo tape. You have told me that you are trying to track down the other band members in the hope of finding a copy of the tape. I don't know if you will succeed in finding it and I'm not sure if it would be worth your while to do so because I have to tell you that I did not write to you thirty-three years ago.

Let me explain. In September 1983, I had an assistant at Polydor called Sabine who was responsible, amongst other things, for the post. We had a disagreement. I can tell you now, as it is so long ago, that I had an affair with Sabine. An affair I had to end. I was obliged to tell her our relationship was over and I was letting her go. She seemed to accept the situation, to take it well, as they say. But, in fact, she didn't take it well, she took it very badly. The day she left, she took her revenge by changing all the letters she sent out. To all those who had sent us a tape before the summer that we had decided to reject, she sent a personalised acceptance letter asking them to contact us for a meeting. After Sabine left, I found myself with almost a hundred people calling me for meetings. I was forced to explain that the letter they had received had been an administrative error. That their tracks were not of interest to us. You can imagine how that went down. Some didn't believe me, and turned up anyway; some were pretty threatening. That lasted for over three weeks, then it settled down and I heard no more of that damned Sabine.

From a distance of more than thirty years, I quite admire the style of Sabine's revenge. And I realise that I probably deserved it. Believe me, I won't forget September 1983 in a hurry.

I recognise my signature diligently forged by Sabine at the bottom of your letter. I'm also sure that she wrote the letter because she always used that turquoise ink, and because, in autumn 1983, there were only two groups and one singer that attracted our interest. We offered those three a meeting, but, of course, they received a rejection letter. I was able to contact them, however, and rectify the situation. Your group, the Holograms, was not one of the two groups contacted.

I am sorry to have to give what may be a disappointing explanation. If it's any consolation, the groups we took on that year did not go on to have successful careers, and nor did the singer. Perhaps we should have taken on the Holograms. Perhaps you were better. The music industry is such a lottery ... Even at sixty-three, and retired from the fray, I am not sure that I always made the best choices.

Yours sincerely
Claude Kalan

Alain was overcome by laughter. The same nervous laughter as in the post office, but this time even more hysterical, and accompanied by the definite feeling that if God existed his sense of humour knew no bounds. He looked down at the USB stick Ivana had brought him and picked it up contemplatively. First there had been vinyl records, then cassettes, CDs, now this: a little piece of plastic smaller than a lighter. Ivana had liked the songs and had even downloaded them to her iPod – which proved that songs produced in the early eighties could appeal to a girl thirty years later. On the other hand, Polydor had not kept their demo, no singles would ever have been produced, no radio station would ever have played the Holograms and 'Such Stuff as Dreams Are Made On' would never have entered the Top 50. Alain wondered if it was actually worth listening to the songs again. Perhaps it would be better for the memory of the songs to be for ever associated with the sunny afternoon they were recorded, when everyone had been young and enthusiastic. Perhaps that was the magic he had been chasing after all these years?

Alain had still not decided what to do when he heard keys in the lock. 'Hello,' called Véronique from the hallway.

She took off her coat, put down her bag and came into the living room. 'I'm exhausted but it was really good; I made some very useful contacts at the exhibition. How was your day?'

Alain looked at the sofa and imagined the outline of Ivana there, but already the lines were blurred, already she had become a distant memory.

'Me?' he said, looking at his wife. 'Nothing much, just home visits.'

Epilogue

Domitile put the finishing touches to her comms strategy for JBM. She called it 'Appearance/Disappearance'. The issue of *Paris Match* featuring JBM had flown off the shelves and the picture from the train station had swiftly 'gone viral'. The cover story, banally but apparently crowd-pleasingly entitled 'JBM, the interview', had led to a 40 per cent boost in sales. Numerous media outlets had got in touch with Domitile asking for another interview, but JBM had suddenly ceased to be available, and disappeared from view for several weeks.

The same pattern repeated itself several times as JBM's popularity rating continued to climb. Then an article in *Le Monde* cranked things up a gear, marking the beginning of the campaign for the queen of comms. A blitzkrieg of a campaign, short and sharp like a flash of lightning, with no one able to stand in its way. Popular philosopher Alain Finkielkraut's instantly famous piece entitled 'Coming full circle' heralded the end of the Fifth Republic and even of the societal model it had upheld since 1958. Few people took the analysis seriously, considering 'Finkie' to have gone a step too far this time. Yet ahead of the article, the newspaper had reproduced the no less notorious piece 'When France becomes bored' by Pierre Viansson-Ponté, published in the same newspaper on 15 March 1968, diagnosing the principal causes of the events that would break out that May. Almost half a century apart, these two thinkers, two men of letters, reason and intellect, had put the world they saw from their windows into words, capturing the zeitgeist before anyone else. JBM had heard about the philosopher's article, and it was probably when he finished reading it for himself that he really began to take on board what Aurore, Blanche and Domitile had said.

The investigation into the attack on the Zénith was fruitless and Vaugan could no longer ensure that FR had any kind of political presence. While the press talked of a 'long road to recovery' for the controversial leader who positioned himself 'To the Right of the Right', the true outlook was even worse: since he had woken from his coma in hospital, Vaugan had given incoherent responses to all the questions his doctors had asked. Among other things, he said his parents and sister should be informed, that he needed to get to work and couldn't be kept in any longer. When asked what his job was, Vaugan answered that he was a carpenter's apprentice. Though it was true he had taken a vocational carpentry course – and passed with flying colours – that was almost thirty years ago. When Vaugan replied, '1985 – why?' to the standard question 'Can you tell me what year it is, Sébastien?' his doctor recommended a period of bed rest. He questioned the young men and the girl in combats who had taken turns to stand at their leader's door since he had come into hospital, asking them to contact Vaugan's next of kin, his *family*. 'We're his family,' one of them replied. 'You may be his political family, but I'm talking about parents, a wife, children,' the doctor countered gently. But Vaugan's parents were long dead, as was his little sister, who had been killed in a boating accident over twenty years earlier. And Vaugan had no wife, no partner, no mistress. One morning, the doctor had to summon the courage to explain to his plaster-bound patient that he was considerably older than twenty and there was nothing and nobody left of the world he thought he was living in.

Paralysed from the waist down, slumped in a wheelchair pushed by his last remaining followers, Vaugan, while still remembering only the odd fragment of his political life, gradually managed to piece together the puzzle of the missing three decades, and came to what he saw as the inevitable conclusion: his lifeless body was found in his office at the Black Billiard. The autopsy revealed that Vaugan had ingested a vial of cyanide of the type carried by special forces on both sides during the Second World War, to be taken if they fell into enemy hands. The press didn't fail to highlight the fact that Vaugan had killed himself in the same way Hermann Göring had done at Nuremberg. Alongside this act of despair – not without its causes – Vaugan had done something else, which didn't make the papers. He had entrusted his solicitor with a will in which he left the sizeable contents of his bank account and the Black Billiard building to the Society for the Protection of Animals, stipulating in writing that he was making the donation because he had 'always loved big dogs'. The organisation never disclosed the legacy to the media. The Black Billiard building, on which work to turn it into the headquarters of France République remained unfinished, was sold to an American pension fund. All that is left of Vaugan today is the family tomb at Juvisy, where a few of his followers gather once a year before heading off to drink beer in memory of the 'commander'.

While Vaugan lay in his hospital bed imagining himself in 1985, the political mainstream continued to prepare for the forthcoming election. Despite his lacklustre record and a popularity rating close to zero, the incumbent announced his intention to stand for the highest office once again. Though some were outraged, most of the party leaders reacted with customary caution and were philosophical about the decision, counting on the party's primaries to put an end to the matter. Against all odds, the current president beat François Larnier by the narrowest of margins. Larnier, who had topped all the internal polls, made a spectacle of himself on the night the results were announced at party headquarters. 'Oh, no! Not him!' he shouted in front of an audience of stunned journalists. 'You mark my words, I will not stand by and watch this happen.' The next day, the two men's lawyers appealed for a recount.

In the weeks following the dispute, some strange anomalies came to light. One of François Larnier's supporters, who had been dead for two years, had nevertheless turned out to vote for his choice of candidate. Other activists who had voted for the president could not be reached at the addresses given on their forms, and had never been seen by their supposed neighbours. The opposition condemned 'grave suspicions of fraud, unworthy of the spirit and values upon which the Republic rests, and which tarnish our very view of France'. The situation was festering on when the president took perhaps the strongest decision of his entire presidency: not to stand. A decision he had 'thought long and hard about, and taken in complete peace of mind', he declared with a strained rictus grin that fooled no one during the short address he made to the nation at eight o'clock one evening, 'in order not to give currency to rumours and lies, to put an end to the harmful atmosphere hanging over public life, and to restore respectful democratic debate to its rightful place at the heart of political life at every level. To the people of France, this is not a goodbye. I shall remain in office as Head of State until the forthcoming election. Long live the Republic; *vive la France*.' Then the president withdrew into silence, and didn't speak again.

François Larnier found himself entrusted, as he had wished, with the mighty task of representing his party at the presidential elections. The opposition, which had no desire to go through the same nightmare and could already sense that its primaries had got off to a bad start, held a meeting at which it was decided by one vote that the primaries would be called off. Meanwhile the Front National continually condemned its adversaries' tricks and strategies, while presenting itself as a model of unity and integrity – the only party capable of rallying round one candidate, without questions needing to be asked of anyone. This was how the political landscape looked when the man who still came top when voters were asked, 'Which person in a position of responsibility is best able to govern France in the years to come?' announced his decision to stand. Politically independent with no party allegiance, surrounded only by a small group going by the name of Union for the Republic, JBM began his campaign.

The very next day, a commentator – quite accurately – compared the political class to 'a flight of crazed and screeching swallows, circling above the garden of France a quarter of an hour before the storm hits'. Descending into panic, none of the parties were able to come out with a clear and measured response to the announcement of this unconventional candidacy. The opposition – now with six candidates, all issuing completely contradictory statements – was displaying almost unprecedented levels of chaos and incompetence. It was becoming ever clearer that no citizen wished to put the country's future, and that of its nuclear force, in the hands of one of these stressed, confused men who no longer even seemed able to answer questions from journalists.

'Underground cabinets' were formed within the parties with the express purpose of smearing JBM, but the Arcadia boss was without a blemish: no lavish work carried out on his offices; no outlandish restaurant bills; no scandalous spending on artworks, private jet bills, obscenely expensive holidays in five-star hotels, hidden bank accounts. As a matter of fact, there were only four things that could be held against him:

– His marriage to a rich woman – but there was no law against this, and his own fortune was not far off that of the Caténac heir.

– His decision to drive an American car, a Lincoln – a matter of taste, and he had paid for it out of his own account, so it was an item of personal property.

– His Breguet chronometer watch – the brand was one of the most respectable around, and the most highly respected by experts. What was more, there were photographs to prove that he had worn the same one for the past twenty years.

– His impressive collection of cufflinks. This innocent obsession could hardly be classed a mortal sin – and barely even a luxury.

Money, scandal, sex, drugs: there was no story.

Though the underground cabinets had a tip-off pointing them towards JBM's brother's theatrically staged suicide in the window of Au Temps Passé, it was mutually agreed, without the need for discussion, that there was no way they were going to bring it up. Not that they felt any particular sense of respect for the dead, but exploiting the tragedy to harm JBM risked backfiring: the suicide of a loved one was no laughing matter.

Whatever the circumstances, an event like that called for silence and compassion. 'We've got nothing, nothing!' despaired one of the leaders of these cabinets. Even Domitile Kavanski, who usually charged a fortune for an hour of her time, had decided to work for him for free since his appearance on *The Big Debate*. The agreement she had signed with JBM was clear: her advice was 'given free of charge and no financial transaction is involved'. As far as she was concerned, entering the history books was enough; it didn't need to come with a cheque.

The same people also tried to dig up dirt on Aurore, but again found nothing to use against her. A young woman from Burgundy whose mother ran a hotel and whose father, who was divorced from the mother and had died five years earlier, had been a wine merchant. A brother who also worked in the wine industry, but at a lower level than his father. Aurore Delfer's brilliant career had led her to JBM. Full stop. Having never brought out an album, the existence of the Holograms escaped their attention completely. Though they had managed to find an impressive number of Aurore's past lovers, a figure that was not in proportion to the length of the relationship – a fact which made many of them salivate over the young blonde – it went no further than that. For a time, they dreamt up the possibility of an affair between JBM and his PA, but, there again, they drew a blank. Ironically enough, one of these reports contained the following line: 'Though their relationship sometimes goes beyond the purely professional according to our sources, the age difference between them means that they have something of a father–daughter dynamic. Nothing untoward, no grounds for attack.'

'We may as well try to open a safe with a toothpick,' a member of one of the underground cabinets summed it up nicely before leaving the room. Almost all the party councillors put discreet feelers out towards the Union for the Republic. Domitile Kavanski sifted out the opportunists and filed their details in one of three folders on her computer: 'Scumbag', 'Dead loss', 'Depends what he can give us'.

JBM didn't hold a single rally – 'old-fashioned, so yesterday, pointless at the national level', according to Domitile – and communicated solely through the press, on TV, radio and online. The time came for the last official polls before the election. The final estimates of the pollsters put him well ahead in the first round of voting, without a clear picture of how the rest of the votes would be spread; the traditional right, left and the FN all seemed to be on level pegging. One thing was for certain: no party could catch JBM after his four-hour phone-in with Jean-Jacques Bourdin on RMC radio which had attracted nine million listeners.

On the night of the first round of the election, newsrooms were buzzing and the atmosphere was electric in television studios, where the presenters exchanged looks, eyes sparkling, as the leading lights of the traditional parties trickled in, pale-faced. Finally, at 7.59 p.m., the countdown to the results began. At exactly eight o'clock, the thunderbolt that struck the Élysée was way more powerful than a 100-million-volt flash of lightning: JBM had been elected in the first round with 50.04 per cent of the votes, blowing apart the political currents that had held sway since the end of the war with the power of a supernova. For the first time in history, there would be no second round of the election. The traditional right, the Front National and the left had finished way behind, in that order but with almost nothing between them, none securing more than 15 per cent of the vote, the variations statistically insignificant. The other parties classified as 'alternative' were left to collect the crumbs.

The Republicans announced their dissolution in the days that followed, and the main leaders of the traditional right retired from politics. The party was reborn at the instigation of the young guard of centrists, under the new name WTC (We The Centrists). Its defining feature was resistance to change. The Socialists decided to change their name and eventually to split into three distinct parties: TSL (The Social Liberals), TL (The Left), and DP (Democracy and Progress), which tore one another to pieces until there was nothing left. Meanwhile, the far right had also taken a beating. A rallying call sent out at a big demonstration had fallen flat and its support gradually dwindled over subsequent years until it had fallen back to the levels of its political beginnings. The streamlined national unity government put in place by JBM got to work and the month after the election set out its vision for a new society. The end of the Fifth Republic was ratified by the Constitutional Council. The Sixth Republic was established that September. A year later, France's economy was growing at the rate of 3.2 per cent and was forecast to exceed 4.7 per cent the following year. 'I'm not a politician, I'm just a link in a chain whose duty is to make a change in society. We're going to do it together. We'll hold on to our values and everything we have defended for centuries, but, for the first time, we're going to face up to the present and the future. Don't be afraid, enjoy the ride.' These were JBM's defining words during the first speech of his first five-year term.

The early days of the Sixth Republic rocked to the sound of a curious song. The craze kicked off in Finland, where a small group of rock fans nostalgic for the eighties got hold of a track that had been posted on a free streaming site the day before and began to share it on social media. Two days later, there were 458 comments in languages as diverse as English, Spanish, Arabic, Portuguese and Chinese on the web page, with no mention of the name of the group or even the song title. Record companies started going into a frenzy at the end of the song's first week online, when – with no music video, only a visual sound wave to accompany it – the track had already been played 17,362,000 times. They contacted pretty much every group imaginable to find out if any of them was the source of the hit song. All were honest enough to reply in the negative.

When, a month later, the song hit ninety-eight million plays, articles began cropping up in newspapers the world over, and a whole array of crazy theories began to circulate on the Net. The most persistent rumour, which went round for several weeks, was that the song was an unreleased David Bowie track, on which the singer's voice had been slightly modified. No sooner had that rumour died down than other theories began to emerge. Some suggested the song could be an unreleased Eurythmics track from the 'Sweet Dreams' era, or an experiment by Giorgio Moroder, who was working with Blondie around that time. Annie Lennox issued a statement via her agent expressing her admiration for the song, but denying the vocals were hers. Likewise Moroder, who praised the melody but claimed not to have written it. More hypotheses flew around: a lost track by Depeche Mode, Propaganda, REM or Roxy Music. Anonymous internet posters even claimed to have been present at the recording. A ghost of the eighties, rock critic Yves Adrien – a music legend whom many were surprised to find was still alive – broke his silence to share his verdict that the song was 'obviously French, really well produced at some point between 1980 and 1984, most likely by an unknown group that broke up years ago and has been lost in the sands of time'.

A giant of the global cyber machine, the teenage dream they had made one fine afternoon in July 1983 now had a life of its own and with every download was born again, becoming ever stronger. No fewer than sixty-seven cover versions were produced around the world. From his home in Thailand, Frédéric Lejeune tried to take the credit for the keyboard playing on the track, but his voice was lost amid the clamour of comments online – and anyone who did notice took him for a fantasist. Bérengère was content to smile to herself whenever the song came on the radio. Stan Lepelle was initially not quite sure how to react, before deciding not to make any comment on a part of his life that risked muddying the waters and detracting from his reputation as a modern artist – in any case, he was too busy working on his upcoming retrospective at MOMA in New York. As for JBM, when asked at a press conference about the hit tune that France and the rest of the world were dancing to, he simply replied with a cat-like smile that there must be something about the song that rang true, that we were all made 'of the stuff of dreams and it's up to us to make those dreams come true'. The camera panned round to the general secretary of the Élysée, Aurore Delfer, and caught her winking knowingly at the president.

Alain had uploaded the song in an internet café thinking people might enjoy it and, crucially, that no one would ever find out where it had come from or who was behind it, nor ever make a centime from it.

That was enough to make him happy.

Reading Group Questions
(Download at www.gallicbooks.com)

A rhapsody, in musical terms, is a free-flowing, emotional piece of music with plenty of variation in tone and structure. Its theme is often about a place. How accurately does this definition fit the novel? What is the effect of the variety of voices included in *French Rhapsody*, and what do they tell us about the state of the French nation today?

To what extent is Antoine Laurain's writing nostalgic for the past?

French Rhapsody delves into the worlds of music and art, both classical and contemporary. How does Laurain weave different art forms together? To what extent is the novel a critique of the modern creative scene?

Can *French Rhapsody* be read as a political novel? What does it tell us about those who long for power?

Antoine Laurain collects antiques and used to work for an antique dealer. His novels often focus around a quest to find a lost object – the talismanic hat in *The President's Hat*, the handbag and the notebook it contains in *The Red Notebook*, the missing demo tape in *French Rhapsody*. What do his novels tell us about the meaning and power of inanimate objects?

A reviewer for French newspaper *Le Figaro* compares Antoine Laurain's comic skill to that of Molière, who understood that even the most absurd or grotesque characters should be likeable. Did you feel any sympathy for Vaugan?

And finally ... would you vote for JBM for president?

The President's Hat
Antoine Laurain
translated by Gallic Books

Dining alone in an elegant Parisian brasserie, accountant Daniel Mercier can hardly believe his eyes when President François Mitterrand sits down to eat at the table next to him.

After the presidential party has gone, Daniel discovers that Mitterrand's black felt hat has been left behind. After a few moments' soul-searching, Daniel decides to keep the hat as a souvenir of an extraordinary evening. It's a perfect fit, and as he leaves the restaurant Daniel begins to feel somehow … different.

ISBN: 9781908313478
e-ISBN: 9781908313577

The Red Notebook
Antoine Laurain
translated by Emily Boyce and Jane Aitken

Bookseller Laurent Letellier comes across an abandoned
handbag on a Parisian street, and feels impelled to
return it to its owner.

The bag contains no money, phone or contact information.
But a small red notebook with handwritten thoughts and
jottings reveals a person that Laurent would very much like to
meet.

Without even a name to go on, and only a few of her
possessions to help him, how is he to find one woman in a city
of millions?

ISBN: 9781908313867
e-ISBN: 9781908313874